# PART ONE

# UNREALITY

Chapter 1


Vickie and Earl were waiting in the motel room and watching 'The Jerry Springer Show' when one of the phones began to ring. There were several phones laid out on the table between them, and each phone had a label taped onto it. The phone labeled 'Nursing Home' was the one that was currently ringing. Vickie waited for Earl to turn the volume down before she answered the phone. "You have reached the Mercy Care Senior Living Facility," she said, using a British accent. "Please listen to the menu carefully, as our options have recently changed. If you know your party's extension, you may dial it at any time.

"For billing, please press 'one'.

"For visiting hours and directions, please press 'two'.

"For the director's office, please press 'three'.

Vickie heard a beep and continued, "Please hold while I connect you to the requested extension."

She waited a few seconds before speaking again, this time in a different accent.

"Dr. Kiley's office," she said. "This is Vanessa speaking. How may I help you?"

"Hello," answered the caller. "My name is Elizabeth Stratton, and I'd like to speak to the director, if possible. I'm trying to obtain a reference for an employee of his, Mrs. Lita Martin. I'm interviewing her for a position as a home health aide for my mother."

"I'm not sure we can give you any information over the phone, Mrs.?"

"Stratton. Elizabeth Stratton. And I'm here with Lita now. She suggested that I call Dr. Kiley. I can have you speak to her yourself, if that would help."

Elizabeth handed the phone to Lita and waited while she spoke to Dr. Kiley's assistant. She hoped she could sort this out today and get back home. She had a good feeling about Lita, and she had been tempted to hire her on the spot. If she lived close enough and could keep an eye on things, she probably would have. But, she knew that her mother's health and well-being would be affected by her choice, so she decided she'd feel safer if she checked Lita's references.

After Lita finished her conversation, she handed the phone back to Elizabeth, and told her that Dr. Kiley would speak to her now. Elizabeth excused herself and brought the phone into another room so she could speak with the director in private. Earl took the phone from Vickie on the other end and introduced himself to Elizabeth.

2

"This is Dr. Kiley," he said. "Can I help you?"

"Yes, Dr. Kiley," Elizabeth answered. "I'm calling for an employee reference for Lita Martin."

"Oh, you must be Elizabeth Stratton," he said. "I've been expecting your call. Lita told me that she was applying for a position as a private nursing aid. I told her that she could have you call me directly.

"I have nothing but good things to say about Lita. she's been one of our most trusted employees for almost twenty years. I was sorry to hear that she was leaving us."

"And do you know why she is leaving?" Elizabeth asked.

"The truth is, Mrs. Stratton, that the job has changed so much that Lita is no longer happy here. We were an independent facility until just recently, when the owners sold out to a corporation. Our new corporate policies are very strict and some of our new rules prevent staff members from getting too friendly with the residents. We're supposed to maintain what they refer to as a 'professional distance'. This new policy, among others, is very difficult for Lita to accept. She's always made a point to become close to those under her care. When she told me she was resigning, I suggested that she look for a position where she could be more of a one-on-one companion."

"That's exactly the type of person I'm looking for," Elizabeth told him. "My mother is not really ill, but she *is* lonely. She can't

3

drive anymore and she really shouldn't be cooking. I'd do those things for her myself, if I lived in the area. I'm supposed to be flying home in two days, so I hoped I could take care of this quickly. I've tried to convince her to come with me… they have some beautiful retirement homes in upstate New York… but she refuses to give up her home."

"I understand your concern," Earl told her, "and if it will help to ease your mind, I highly recommend Lita for the position. It sounds like a perfect match."

"Thank you, Dr. Kiley," Elizabeth said. "You've given me all the information that I need to make my decision."

"You're welcome," he answered. "And I hope you have a safe trip home."


Earl tossed the phone back on the table and turned to Vickie.

"Vanessa?" he asked.

"Yeah, I like the name. I thought I'd try it on for a while," she told him.

"But the nursing home assistant is always 'Vera'," he said. "You're supposed to stick to the script."

"It's just a name," Vickie said. "It's not a big deal."

"But it is a big deal," Earl answered. "You're supposed to stick to the script. You going off script is what screwed up the last job."

"Oh, come on, Earl," she answered. "We had already made a lot of money on that job."

"But we could have made a lot more, Vickie. And we could have avoided having more warrants to hide from."

"So we can never go back to East Overshit, Utah again." she snapped. "That's no great loss, in my opinion."

"That's not the point," he shot back. "From now on, you stick to the script."

"Or what, Earl?" She asked him ."Are you going to tell my mother on me?"

"I might," he answered.

"I don't think so, Earl," she told him. "Because if you do, I might have to tell her our secret."

"You wouldn't do that," he said, confidently. "She'd kill you if she found out."

"No, she wouldn't," Vickie told him. "She expects it from me. Me, she'd forgive. You wouldn't be so lucky, though. She'd cut your balls off while you were sleeping and she'd be three states away before you could crawl to your phone and call 911. But don't worry… I don't plan on telling her. Unless you piss me off."

Lettie came strolling into the motel room about an hour later carrying a bottle of champagne. "Were celebrating tonight," she told them. "I got the job."

"Great news, Lettie," Earl told her. "I like this town. I wouldn't mind staying here a while."

"Jesus, Earl," she hissed, "it's Lita. L I T A. I told you we have to use the right names, even when we're alone. We can't have any more slip-ups."

Earl shot Vickie a smug look before asking Lettie, "So what does the job require? And, more importantly, how much money does the old lady have?"

"She doesn't really need much care, thank God," Lettie answered. "I don't have to bathe her or feed her or anything like that. I'm basically a paid companion. I have to make her meals on the housekeeper's day off and make sure she has some microwavable food for the weekend. I'm supposed to show up around 8:00 am and I can leave after she has her dinner, around 5:00 pm."

"And how much money does she have?" Earl asked again.

"Tons," Lettie said, "if her home is any indication. She lives in a huge house and it's loaded with antiques. And the best part is that her only child, a daughter, is an uptight, guilt-ridden bitch who lives in New York City. I get the impression that she doesn't visit much, either.

"The only downside is that she has a full-time housekeeper who runs the show and handles the purse strings. We'll have to find a way to get rid of her and replace her with Vickie. I'm sure we'll figure it out."

"Can I be 'Vanessa'?" Vickie asked her mother.

"Sure. Use whatever name you want," she answered. "Just make sure you don't slip up. And I think you should practice your southern accent."

Chapter 2


Lettie began her position as Lita, companion to Mrs. Rebecca Morris, two days after her interview. Other than preparing an occasional meal and driving her patient to her various appointments, there wasn't much to do. Rebecca Morris was a docile and lonely old woman who preferred to occupy her time reminiscing about the past while drinking tea. Lita would prepare her tea each afternoon and then sit with her for hours while pretending to be interested in her stories. Rebecca also loved to have her hair brushed and Lita was happy to oblige her several times a day. When Elizabeth made her weekly phone calls to her mother each Sunday, Rebecca had nothing but praises for her new paid companion. Elizabeth hung up after each call feeling confident that she had made the right decision in hiring Lita.

Lettie waited until she felt sure that she had Rebecca's trust before she began her campaign to get rid of the housekeeper, Theresa. When Rebecca started opening up to her about her strained relationship with her daughter, Lettie knew that she had become more than a companion to Rebecca. She had become her friend. And just like friends often do when they're having tea together, she began to gossip. She started making comments and asking questions designed to cause Rebecca to be suspicious of Theresa.

"Do you think she's here legally?" she'd ask. Or, "Did you see the man that picked her up yesterday? I didn't like the looks of him, did you?"

It worked. Eventually Rebecca became so suspicious of Teresa that when a pair of Rebecca's earrings turned up in the pocket of the housekeeper's coat, she terminated her on the spot. She would have gone even further, if Lita hadn't convinced her not to call the police.

"It's her word against ours," Lita told her. "And who knows what lengths her people will go to to keep us quiet. I'd be worried about your safety."

When Elizabeth called the next Sunday, Rebecca gave her the news about Theresa's firing.

"I'll call an agency for a replacement," Elizabeth told her."I'll set up some interviews for the end of next week. I can't get there before then."

"You don't have to," Rebecca responded. "Lita and I took care of it ourselves. My new housekeeper, Vanessa, started yesterday and I believe she's going to work out fine."

Elizabeth hung up feeling relieved that she had found someone so completely capable like Lita to take care of her mother. *She really is a godsend,* Elizabeth thought to herself.

Lita/Lettie and Vanessa/Vickie took good care of Rebecca Morris for several months, until they had the full trust and confidence of both Rebecca and her daughter. Then they started drugging her. Occasionally at first... just enough to convince her that her memory was beginning to fail and that she was losing periods of time. Just enough to convince her that it wasn't safe for her to be left alone.

Rebecca told her daughter about her 'episodes' on one of her weekly phone calls and informed her that Lita had agreed to move in and become her full-time live-in employee. She had to increase her salary, of course, but it was well worth it to be able to stay in her own home. And Lita coordinated with Vanessa, the new housekeeper, to make sure that Rebecca was never, ever left alone.

Elizabeth was surprised by the news and asked her mother if she could speak privately with Lita.

"What's going on with my mother?" Elizabeth asked her when Lita came on the line.

"She's been having more episodes lately and I don't feel right leaving her alone," Lita answered.

"And for how long has she been having these episodes? Elizabeth asked.

"As long as I've been here," Lita told her. "I just assumed you knew about them and that they were the reason why she needed a companion."

"And why would you assume that I knew?"

"Well, she *is* your mother," Lita answered.

"But she seemed fine the last time I visited," Elizabeth replied. "And she always seems fine when I talk to her over the phone."

"Didn't you notice how disoriented she seemed the last time you called?" Lita asked her.

"No, not really." Elizabeth answered. "She seemed like her normal self."

"Oh," Lita said, sounding surprised ."I'm surprised you didn't notice."

"I think I'll call her doctor tomorrow," Elizabeth told her.

"That's a good idea," Lita agreed. "You really should become more involved. If you have a pen handy I'll give you the number for her new doctor."

"Why does she have a new doctor? What happened to Dr. Shea?"

"It's Dr. Piche" Lita corrected her. "And Dr. Piche recommended that she see a doctor that specializes in cases like hers."

"What do you mean by 'cases like hers'? Elizabeth asked her. "And no, I don't have a pen handy."

"You really should talk to the doctor," Lita answered. "His name is Dr. Early, and I'll text you his number as soon as we hang up."

When their conversation ended, Lettie hung up the phone and called Vickie into the room.

"I just got off the phone with Elizabeth," she told her. "She'll probably be calling Dr. Early first thing tomorrow morning, so make sure you rehearse tonight."

"Okay," Vickie answered. "I think I'll give Dr. Early's receptionist an Indian accent and name her 'Vareena'."

Chapter 3


"Good morning.This is Dr. Early's office, Vareena speaking. How may I help you, please?"

"Good morning, Vareena. My name is Elizabeth Stratton and my mother, Rebecca Morris is a patient of Dr. Early's. I'd like to speak with the doctor, if I may."

"I'm sorry," Vareena answered, "but he's not in the office at this time. Is there something I can help you with? Would you like to leave a message?"

"Are you familiar with my mother's case?" Elizabeth asked.

"Yes, I've met your mother. She's a lovely woman.She came in a few weeks ago for the first time with her companion, Mrs. Martin. Also a lovely woman."

"Well, can you tell me what she's being treated for… What her diagnosis is?"

"No," Vareena answered. "I'm sorry, but I can't do that. The HIPAA law forbids me from giving out that information."

"But I'm her daughter!" Elizabeth replied.

"Oh, I understand your concern. But the law is the law and without Mrs. Stratton's or Mrs. Martin's written consent, I can't release any medical information."

"Mrs. Martin? Why does Mrs. Martin have that kind of authority?" Elizabeth asked.

"Dr. Early suggested that your mother give 'power of attorney' to someone who would be available in an emergency, just in case someone had to make a decision for her in a timely manner. Your mother chose Mrs. Martin."

"But why would someone have to make a decision for her? Why wouldn't she be making her own decisions?"

"Well, because sometimes your mother is… um… unable to make her own decisions. I'm sure you're aware of your mother's condition and why there's a need for…."

Elizabeth cut her off and said, "I think I'd better speak with Dr. Early. Will you please have him return my call?"

"Of course, Mrs. Stratton. But if you'd like to talk to him before he returns to the office, you can reach him later this morning at your mother's house. She has a 10:00 am appointment."

"He makes house calls?" Elizabeth asked.

"Yes, Vareena answered. "But only for those patients who are apt to become agitated or disoriented when leaving their familiar surroundings."

Vickie laced Rebecca's scrambled eggs with hydrocodone the next morning. Not enough to knock her out, but enough to make her a little loopy. When Elizabeth phoned at 10:00 AM she noticed that her mother **did** sound confused and disoriented. When their conversation was over, she asked Rebecca to let her speak to Dr. Early. When he came on the line, she asked him what was going on.

"Well, as her daughter, I know that you are certainly aware of her condition. Mrs. Martin told me how close you two are. I'm sure that, given the situation, you must be very relieved to have her as your mother's caretaker. She does a marvelous job, and it's not an easy one. Unfortunately, your mother's condition is deteriorating much faster than Dr. Piche expected. That's why he referred her to my office."

When Elizabeth expressed concern that Lita, rather than she, had 'power of attorney', Dr. Early told her that he understood how she felt.

"I'll ask your mother's housekeeper to call her attorney and request new paperwork," he told her. "Just let Vanessa know when you'll be available to come in and sign them."

"Can't they just email them to me?" she asked.

"No," he told her. "You have to sign them in person in the attorney's office. You'll need two witnesses, too."

"Oh" Elizabeth said. "I didn't realize that. I'm not sure when I'll have the chance to make that trip again. I guess that's not the major priority right now. As long as you're comfortable with Lita making decisions for her, I guess it will be okay until I can arrange to fly out. The important thing is my mother's health."

There were no more tea parties for Rebecca after that phone call. Lita stopped brushing her hair and Vickie stopped cooking. Her meals were now either canned soup or fast food, usually sprinkled with enough drugs to keep her asleep most of the time. While Rebecca slept Lettie, Vickie and Earl ate out almost every night using Rebecca's credit cards to pay for their meals. They were having dinner at one of their favorite restaurants one night when Earl informed them that he had finished studying Rebecca's financial records and he had a pretty good idea of her net worth.

"So, what's she worth?" Vickie asked.

"Somewhere around five to six million," he told them.

"Wow," Becky said ."I knew she had money but I didn't expect it to be that much."

"Let's go shopping!" Lettie cried. "We'll finish our meals and head for the mall. We've earned ourselves a nice reward."

"I can't go tonight," Vickie announced. "I have a date."

"Then we'll go tomorrow morning," Lettie said.

"What about Rebecca?" Earl asked.

"We'll give her an injection," Lettie answered. "We'll give her enough to knock her out for hours. We'll do some shopping and then go somewhere for a nice lunch. She'll never even know we're gone."

Lettie and Earl were having coffee the next morning, waiting for Vickie to finish getting ready for their shopping trip when Earl said, "I hope she hurries up. I gave Rebecca her shot about an hour ago. I thought we'd be leaving before now."

Lettie was about to reply when Vickie walked into the kitchen and said, "I hope you two are ready to go because I already took care of Rebecca."

"What do you mean 'took care of'?" Earl asked.

"I gave her a shot," she answered

"But I gave her a shot ten minutes ago," Lettie said.

"And I gave her one, too," Earl told her.

"Go check on her, Earl," Lettie told him.

"Why do I have to do it?" he asked.

"Go, Earl. Now!" she demanded."

"No," Earl told her. "I'm not going in there."

Vickie turned and left the room and went to check on Rebecca while Lettie and Earl waited at the kitchen table.

"She's dead," Vickie told them when she returned. "What do we do now?"

"Oh my god!" Earl exclaimed. "Dead? You killed her!"

"No," Vickie said. "*We* killed her. It was an accident, though, so it's not like we murdered her."

"Oh my god!" Earl repeated. "Murder! I don't want to be a murderer. This isn't just a petty scam now. We could go away for life, if we get caught. I don't know if I can handle this, Lettie. What the hell are we going to do?"

Earl was starting to panic. He rambled on and on about what the consequences could be, should they be caught, and kept insisting that he didn't want to be a murderer.

"Oh, calm down, Earl," Lettie told him. She was getting impatient with his histrionics. "It's not the end of the world. We can handle this."

"But what are we going to do?" he asked again.

"We're going to put on the wigs and the sunglasses," Lettie answered. "We'll grab all the debit and credit cards that Vickie has pin numbers for and we'll hit as many ATMs as we can. And then we get out of town fast."

"Where are we going to go? Earl asked her.

"I've been thinking of relocating to LA for a while now," she answered.

"Good idea," Earl said. "Is your sister still there? Maybe she can help us get started."

"Oh, I doubt if she can help us with anything," Lettie said. "She can barely help herself. But we'll be able to stay with her until we feel safe enough to start a new job."

Lettie instructed Earl and Vickie to don their disguises, pack their bags and load up the car with as many of Rebecca's belongings as they could fit.

"Vickie, you're going to have to teach me and Earl how to speak with a british accent during the drive to LA," she told her daughter.

"Why?" Vickie asked.

"Because I got an idea I'm working on. If we can pull this off, we can make some real money.  In fact, if it works like I'm hoping it will, we'll be able to retire. I'm thinking we should go someplace where it's warm and where there's no extradition treaty with the U.S."

Chapter 4

Vickie visited four different agencies on Monday morning before she found one that she liked. The office had a small, but expensively furnished waiting area. The receptionist sat in a well-padded chair, upholstered in a soft beige leather behind a huge mahogany desk. There were plush, beige armchairs for visitors arranged around a glass coffee table, all sitting on a vividly-colored oriental carpet atop highly-polished hardwood floors. A quick glance told Vickie everything she needed to know about the agency: it served the very rich.

The receptionist seemed overwhelmed. She was talking on the phone and had at least one other call on hold. As soon as she finished on one line, another line would begin to ring. There didn't appear to be anybody else in the office, so Vickie took a seat in one of the armchairs and waited for an opportunity to speak to the receptionist. She was checking her phone for messages when the receptionist summoned her.

"Can I help you?" she asked.

"I sure hope so," Vickie answered in her best country-girl accent. She flashed a college ID card at the other woman and told her she was a student at the university.

"My name is Violet," she told her, "and I'm working on a paper comparing the quality of healthcare for senior citizens in facilities versus private homes. And I was hoping to job-shadow a receptionist in an agency that provides home healthcare."

"I'm not really the receptionist," the woman told her. "My name is Debby, and I'm the office manager. Our receptionist is on vacation, so I'm filling both positions right now. I'd love to help you out, but I've got my hands full this week. Maybe if you come back in a couple of weeks..."

"But I can help you!" Vickie exclaimed. "I'd be willing to spend a week as an unpaid intern. I did that at a nursing home for a week and I learned so much more than I would have just by watching someone. I could answer your phone for you or ……"

The interview was interrupted again by two phone lines ringing at once.

"Which nursing home did you intern at?" Debby asked when she finally got a break from the phone. "I know a lot of the staff members at most of them."

"Oh, it was back home in Kentucky," Vickie answered, "during spring break. But I can get you the name and number of the woman I worked for, if you'd like a reference."

Three phone lines began ringing simultaneously and Debby had to halt their conversation to attend to business. Vickie studied her closely while she waited. Vickie was always looking for inspiration for new characters that she could play and she thought that Debby's would be a fun persona to adopt. She took note of her appearance: cream linen slacks with an olive green, silk safari-type blouse. She had on gold strappy sandals and a few pieces of gold jewelry. Her nails were short and painted a buff color. Vickie decided from her accent that she was probably from New York. To Vickie, she looked and sounded like a typical New York career woman, and Vickie stored the information in her memory for later use.

Vickie also noticed that Debby was beginning to lose her patience while trying to handle the frequent phone calls. She hoped that Debby's frustration would work in her favor. She was right. During a short break in the phone calls, Debby turned to her and asked, "When can you start?"

Debby spent a little over an hour training Vickie for her receptionist duties. She gave her an information sheet that listed the services they provided, along with the prices they charged. Vickie was to fill out a form on the computer for each call that came in from someone in need of a nurse or healthcare aide. She filled in the necessary information and forwarded each form to Debby, who would then check the roster and assign the jobs. Whoever received the assignment would log their hours on another online form. Debby paid them by direct deposit. It was all done online and none of the nurses or aides ever visited the office. Debby had her own office behind the reception area, so Vickie was alone for most of the day.

The call that Vickie was waiting for came on Thursday. The caller was a secretary from an attorney's office. She was calling to hire a full-time nurse for one of their clients. She explained to 'Violet' that he was a wealthy shut-in who had outlived most of his immediate family and had no contact with whatever relatives were still alive.

"He's very... um...*difficult*," the woman admitted. "He's fired four nurses so far. The agency that we normally use won't send another one. They won't even take my calls."

"I think I can help you," Vickie told her. "We actually have a nurse on call who specializes in difficult cases. Her name is Letitia Marlen, and I happen to know that she's available. She doesn't work for us directly, however, because she freelances for a few different agencies. But she still has to have all the qualifications that we require for our staff. Our employees have to have a certain level of education and experience, along with impeccable references to be allowed to represent us. Letitia meets all of our criteria. The only difference is, that instead of paying us, you'll pay her directly.

"Would you like me to set up an interview?"

"A phone interview will do," the secretary answered her. "Just have her call me ASAP and I'll give her the details."

"Great," Vickie answered. "I'm sure you'll be as happy with Letitia as her former patients have been. I just have a few questions that I need for our records," she continued. "Is it a live-in position?"

"Yes," the secretary answered. "Is that a problem?"

"No, not at all," Vickie said. "I just need the names of anyone else residing in the household."

"He lives alone," she told her. "There's a full-time maid Monday through Friday, and a part-time one on the weekend. They're only there during the day. They leave after he has his dinner. They're the only two people he has any contact with, other than my boss, who only sees him a few times a year."

*Perfect* thought Vickie.

# PART TWO

# JOE

# Chapter 5

Joe was sitting on the couch, watching the Golf Channel and sharing a bag of
chips with Fleur when Corinne walked in.

"You know the vet said she's not supposed to be eating junk food."

"Hi, babe. I didn't hear you come in. And I only gave her a couple, I swear."

" Well, don't give her any more and, please ditch the bathrobe and put some clothes on. I'm tired of seeing you in that robe."

"What's the point in getting dressed?" Joe asked. "It's not like I can go anywhere."

"The kitchen designer is coming today. If you want to have some say in the design, then you need to put some clothes on. And make sure you wear a pair of pants that covers your ankle bracelet."

"Okay. I'm bored enough to be looking forward to meeting with her. I already know what kind of look I want... black granite counters, stainless steel appliances and maybe maple cabinets and black marble floor..."

"No," Corinne stopped him.

"What do you mean, no?"

"I've already picked out the cabinets. Lori's bringing over one of the doors, so that we can check the finish and give the okay before they complete the order."

"How come you picked them out without me?"

"Because you couldn't go to the showroom with me. Lori sure can't lug cabinet samples over here."

"I guess you're right. I don't really care, as long as we get nice shiny black granite countertops."

"No granite," Corinne told him. " The perimeter counters will be dark butcher block and the island will have white marble."

"We don't have an island."

"We will."

"So why don't we put black marble on it to match the floor?"

"Because the floor is going to be hard wood."

"But we're getting stainless steel appliances, right?"

"The appliances will be covered with panels that match the cabinets. Except for the oven. We can get a stainless steel oven."

"So why are we meeting with Lori if you've already picked everything out?"

"She's bringing paint and fabric samples, plus tile samples for the backsplash. Oh, and the cabinet door."

"Honestly, Cor, it doesn't sound worth putting on pants for."

"Go," Corinne answered. "And please shave and shower, too. She'll be here any minute."

When Joe came back downstairs, Corinne and Lori were sitting at the kitchen table, flipping through fabric samples. Joe sat down and Corinne handed him a small cabinet door.

"Here's what the cabinets are going to look like. What do you think?"

"Can I wipe it off? See what it looks like when it's clean?" Joe asked.

"It is clean," Lori told him. "That's a special glazed finish they apply to make them look aged."

"It just looks like dirt to me," he said. "Besides, we've got a whole kitchen full of aged cabinets. That's why we're remodeling."

Corinne rolled her eyes and said, "That's the finish I chose, Joe. I like it. And since when do you care so much about the kitchen?"

"Of course I care. It's my kitchen, too. I spend a lot of time in here, probably even more than the maid does."

"Okay, Joe. Then answer one question for me without turning around: What color are the curtains?"

Joe returned to the family room, turned the Golf Channel back on and went to work on the bag of chips. He wasn't really all that interested in kitchen design, anyway. Mostly he was just bored.

Joe went looking for Corinne after he heard Lori leave.

"Let's get Maria to make us some lunch, Cor. We can eat out on the patio together. It's a beautiful day."

"Every day is beautiful here," she answered. "but Maria won't be here for lunch. She has class this afternoon, remember? You're babysitting Alfie."

"I still don't understand why we're sending our maid to college. We're already paying for Kara's tuition, and we'll be paying Jojo's in a couple of years, too."

"It's just part-time, Joe. It doesn't cost us that much. And she's got A's in both of her classes! You should be proud of her for trying to build a better life for her and Alfie. She doesn't want to be a maid forever."

"She's barely one now," he answered. "And it's nice to hear that she's working hard *somewhere.* She's hardly ever here. Why do we have a live-in maid anyway?"

"Because she needed a place to live. You saw where she was living, Joe. It wasn't a safe neighborhood for her and Alfie. I worried about them every time I dropped them off. I worried about myself, too, just driving through that neighborhood."

"And if you hadn't insisted on driving your maid home from work, you wouldn't have had to worry.

"And why am *I* babysitting for the maid's son?" he asked.

"Because her sister couldn't watch him today and she doesn't have anybody else. Besides, what else have you got to do?"

"Why can't you watch him?" he asked.

"Because the duchess invited me to tea this afternoon."

"You can't cancel? Say something came up?"

"I don't want to cancel, Joe. Since the duchess started inviting all the neighborhood women to her teas, I've finally gotten to meet some of them. None of them refuse her invitations, because they feel important rubbing elbows with a duchess. I only go because it's the first chance I've had to have any kind of a social life here.

"And that's another reason I like having Maria and Alfie here. You were so busy at work when we first moved here, that you were hardly ever home. And the kids were spending most of their time with their new friends. I was lonely."

"Yeah, but you've got friends here now."

"Friends? They're hardly friends, Joe. If the duchess dropped me tomorrow, so would the others. There was one neighborhood woman, Tara, who came to our first two get-togethers. The last time she was there, she asked the duchess if we could have a tour of the house. The duchess got real snippy and told her that we were in her *home*, and that if she wanted a tour, she should go to a museum. Tara never got invited back."

"Your duchess sounds like a bitch,' Joe said.

"She kind of is," Corinne agreed.

"I'm sorry, Cor", Joe told her. " I wish, for your sake, that the neighbors here were friendlier."

"Don't be sorry, Joe. I wanted to move here just as much as you did."

"I know. But maybe it's my fault that you haven't been able to make friends. Maybe they don't want to associate with someone who's married to a pimp."

"You're not a pimp."

"I know that and you know that, but do they?"

Corinne sighed. "Joe, you're from Jersey. You're Italian. You hang around all day in a bathrobe and you're under house arrest. They think you're a friggin' real-life Tony Soprano! You know Shawna? The blonde with the lips that look like they're ready to burst? Well, her husband is in prison for embezzlement. And Nicole? The real tall one that looks like she had all the fat sucked out of her thighs and injected into her ass? Her husband's a criminal attorney under indictment for money-laundering.

"Having a convicted criminal for a husband is about the only thing that I have in common with these women."

Joe shook his head, and said, "But I'm not really a criminal."

"They don't have to know that, Joe."

Joe had to agree with Corinne about the neighbors. They weren't the most friendly folks. He barely even knew most of them. *Everyone* knew each other in their old neighborhood. There were always kids outside playing together and people riding bikes or walking their dogs. There were never people on the sidewalks here, and if there had been, he wouldn't be able to see them from his house anyway. It sure did make him feel isolated sometimes, especially when he couldn't travel more than 200 yards from his front door.

He missed being able to come and go as he pleased, and he really missed going to his office. Luckily, he had enough money put away to live on until his confinement was over, but then what? The police had seized his business property, so he'd have to work from home and build his business up all over again. He wasn't really worried. He knew he'd manage somehow. In the meantime, though, he still had sixteen months of house arrest to complete.

While Corinne was getting ready to go see the duchess, Maria came in with Alfie. She handed Joe a paper sack of burgers and fries and said, "Here's lunch. I've got to run or I'll be late."

"Thanks, Maria," he told her, sarcastically. "You didn't have to do that."

"You owe me $12.47," she answered.

After they had finished their burgers, Joe and Alfie went into the family room to watch movies. Joe made it all the way through 'The Lion King', but he couldn't keep his eyes open during 'Frozen'. Corinne found both of them snoring on the couch when she got back. She shook Joe until he woke up.

"Oh, hi, Corinne. I must have just dozed off. How was your tea party?"

"It was nice."

"So what do you do at a tea party?' he asked.

"Well, we talked about putting together a fundraising event for a girl's school that the duchess is building somewhere in Africa. And we drank tea and ate scones."

"Scones, huh?", I've never had a scone. What do they taste like?"

"Kind of like a muffin, but with all the flavor and moisture sucked out. But the duchess loves them. I guess it's a British thing."

"Are you sure she's on the up?" Joe asked. "I mean, are you sure she's really a duchess?"

"Of course I am, Joe. Why would you even think such a thing?"

"I don't know, Cor. I just get a funny feeling about her. Like maybe she's a phony."

"Joe, she has all kinds of pictures of herself with members of the royal family. She even has one with her and Pippa."

"Who the hell is Pippa?", Joe asked.

"She's Kate Middleton's sister!"

"And who the hell is Kate Middleton?"

"She's the girl who married Prince William. The duchess was at the wedding."

"Pictures can be faked, Corinne. It doesn't prove anything."

"What about the house, Joe?  That house must be worth millions."

"Maybe she rents," he offered.

"And can you imagine what the rent on that place would be? Geez, Joe, why are you so overly suspicious?"

"I'm not overly suspicious, Corinne. I'm just a better judge of character than you."

"Oh, really? So, tell me again about that nice young filmmaker that you rented a studio to last year….the one who told you he made instructional videos….

"Cor…." Joe tried to stop her, but she wouldn't be stopped.

"You know...the one who turned out to be a porn producer? The one who was running a whorehouse out of your office after hours?

"And what about all those girls that he hired? I think you described them as 'a nice group of young actresses working hard on their careers'? Remember how those 'nice young actresses' protected that sleazebag and testified in court that *you* were their boss?"

Joe threw up his arms and said, "Okay. I get your point."

"Good," she answered. "I have to go pick Jojo up from school and take him to the orthodontist. He's got a game at 6:30, so we'll be going to the ballpark from there. Kara's got a prom-planning meeting after school and then she's going to meet us at the park. We'll all grab burgers or something at the snack bar, so you're on your own until we get home. We should be back around 8:30."

"What's Maria got planned for dinner tonight?", Joe asked her.

"Geez, Joe. It's just you. Can't you fix yourself something?"

"And what exactly am I paying a maid for?"

"She's been running all day, Joe. Give her a break."

"Okay, fine." he said. "I'll order myself a pizza."

"Great idea," she answered sarcastically. "Why don't you do that? Order a whole pizza for yourself, put your bathrobe back on, plop on the couch and stuff yourself while you watch grown men hit balls with sticks!"

"What do you want me to do, Corinne?"

"I don't know, Joe. I just wish you'd do *something*."

Corinne wasn't alone in wishing Joe would do something. Joe *wanted* to do something. In fact, Joe wanted to do a lot of things and none of them included being stuck in his house. He missed driving Jojo around to his games and practices. It was about the only chance he got to spend time with him. Now that he was a teenager, Jojo was more interested in being with his friends. He missed spending time with Kara, too. She was hardly ever around anymore, now that she had her own car. He hadn't noticed how seldom either of the kids were home when he was busy with work. He understood how Corinne felt. At least Corinne could go to their games and concerts. Kara would be graduating next month and going off to college in the fall, and Joe wouldn't be able to be there to watch her walk across the stage and receive her diploma.

Corinne just didn't understand how hard the situation was for him.

When Corinne and the kids got home from the ballpark, Joe was sound asleep on the couch, in his bathrobe and with an empty pizza box on his lap.

Chapter 6

Joe made sure that he was up early the next morning, and that he had showered, shaved and put on jeans and a t-shirt before joining Corinne and the kids for breakfast. He sat down at the table and Maria set a plate of eggs in front of him. He asked Jojo questions about his baseball game the night before while they ate. After the kids left for school, Corinne and Joe went outside to sit at the patio table where Maria served them their morning coffee.

"How come she acts like a maid when you're home and like a houseguest when you're not?" Joe asked after Maria had returned inside.

"Don't start, Joe. We're lucky to have her," Corinne answered.

Joe decided to change the subject. "So, tell me, Cor, were you happy when you saw me this morning?"

"I'm always happy to see you. What's so special about this morning?"

"I got dressed!"

Corinne sighed. "It's nice to see you ditch the robe, but putting on clothes is hardly an accomplishment."

"I've got an idea," Joe said, changing the subject once more. "Why don't we watch a movie together today? We could make some popcorn and snuggle on the couch."

"So you switched out the robe for clothes and now you want to switch out the dog for me? How is that much different than what you do everyday? And, as tantalizing as that sounds, I can't. I have a meeting with Jojo and his guidance counselor. We're planning his class schedule for next year. Then I have to go pick up Kara's prom dress from the seamstress, do some grocery shopping and stop at the drugstore."

"Why can't Maria do some of those things?" he asked.

"She's not really a personal assistant, Joe."

"She's not really a maid, either, Corinne."

"I'll tell you what," Corinne said, "I should be back around noon. I'll have Maria make us a nice lunch and we can eat together on the patio."

"That sounds good," he answered. "And maybe we can do something together after lunch. It doesn't have to be a movie. Maybe we could play cards, or go swimming."

"I can't. I have a meeting with the charity committee after lunch."

"What charity committee?"

"I told you about it, Joe. The Duchess organized a charity committee with the neighborhood women."

"Yeah, right," he said. "I've been thinking about our conversation yesterday, and I think I know why I feel like something's fishy about your duchess. I know I only met her once, but I could swear that she looks familiar to me, like I've seen her somewhere before."

"Well, I wouldn't be surprised if you have," Corinne told him. "She's a very famous personality in England. I'm sure her picture has been in newspapers and magazines."

"I've had my picture in newspapers, too," Joe reminded her.

"Yeah, I know. But yours was a mugshot," she shot back.

"Yeah, that's kinda my point, Cor."

Joe and Fleur were sitting on the couch, sharing a bag of microwave popcorn and watching a *Seinfield* rerun when he spotted the gardener, Miguel, riding the lawnmower past the window. He decided to go out and talk to him about planting some new shrubs. Joe didn't really care one way or the other about shrubs, but it was the only excuse he could come up with for interrupting him. He walked out the front door, and waved his arms until he was spotted. As the mower came closer, Joe realized that the driver wasn't Miguel after all, but his son, Will. Will was a college student who worked with his father from time to time.

Will stopped the mower and came over to Joe. "Hey, Mr. B. What can I do for you?" he asked.

"Is your dad around?" Joe asked.

"No," he answered. "He had a dentist appointment, so I'm filling in for him today."

"It looks like you're doing a good job, too," Joe told him. "I guess you inherited your father's talent. I suppose you'll be going into business with him when you finish school."

"No, not me," he answered. "I don't want to be a gardener. I plan on being a television personality."

"What do you mean by a 'television personality'?," Joe asked.

"Well, eventually I'd like to have my own late-night talk show, like Jimmy Fallon or Conan. But I have to build a resume first. I might have to start as a radio d.j., you know… build up a listener base. Then I'll try to get a gig hosting a primetime game show or talent show. That's my plan."

"Those jobs aren't easy to get. I hope you have a backup plan."

"Yeah. I might like to be a producer. I'm taking a class this fall where I have to produce a TV pilot."

"By yourself?"

"No, it's a team project."

"What's your pilot going to be about?"

"I don't know yet." Will answered. "Our team is getting together tonight to toss around some ideas."

"Already?" Joe asked. "Don't you have a couple of months before school starts again?"

"Yeah, but we could pick our teams when we signed up for the class, if we wanted to. The school has equipment that they'll loan us, but they don't have a lot and there's always a waiting list. So they give us the whole summer to get started."

"Hey," said Joe, "I might be able to help you out. I've got some stuff stored in the detached garage that you might be able to use. Would you like to take a look?"

"Sure," answered Will.

There was a three-car garage at the end of the driveway and a detached one-car garage set at an angle to the left. The detached garage also had a second floor with a small efficiency apartment. The extra garage was one of the features that had attracted Joe to the property. It was the perfect size to convert into storage for his equipment. He had never liked to leave more than he needed at the studio, in case there was a fire or theft. It turned out to be a smart decision.

"Wow, Mr. B, this is amazing."

Will was looking through the storage cabinets that Joe had hired a carpenter to build to house his collection of equipment.

"I've never even seen cameras like some of the ones you've got. And look at all these different types of mics! We could film day or night, inside or outside, with any size cast we want. This sure gives us a lot of options."

"Yeah, said Joe. "I hate to see it all just sitting here. I trust you, Will. As long as you give me your word that you'll take good care of it, you can use whatever you need."

"You've got my word, Mr. B. And you don't have to worry about the rest of the crew. Having the chance to work with all this stuff will be like Christmas morning to them. We'll take good care of it. I promise."

When Corinne came home for lunch, Joe told her about his conversation with Will.

"I might have to teach them how to use some of the stuff, though. Some of it's a little more high-tech than what they're used to.

"At least it will give me something to do," he added.

"If you really want something to do," she answered, "you could start packing up the kitchen. The contractors are coming the day after tomorrow. There are plenty of boxes in the pantry."

"How long are they gonna be here, Cor?" he asked.

"Two to three weeks," she answered.

"So what do we do for cooking and eating while they're here?"

"We'll stock that little kitchenette over the garage with the basics…"

"You mean the one in the *maid's* quarters?"

"Knock it off, Joe. You know that studio apartment is too small for Maria and Alfie. But it will be big enough for her to fix breakfast and lunch. I guess we'll have to eat out for dinner most nights."

"Well, what about me, Corinne? I can't go out to eat."

"Don't worry… we'll bring the leftovers home."


After Corinne had left for her meeting with the duchess and her charity committee, Joe wandered out to the garage to take an inventory of his audio and video equipment. He figured it might come in handy for Will and his crew. It might help them plan their shoot better if they knew what they had to work with. He was looking forward to helping them with their project. He was also dreading the noise and chaos that would soon begin with kitchen remodel, and having something to occupy some of his time might help him get through it.

Joe had taken up photography as a hobby when he was eight years old. He had received an inexpensive pocket camera for Christmas that year, and he was hooked. He was thirteen when he got his first recording camera. It was a Beta Max, given to him by an uncle who had upgraded to a video cassette camera.

Joe and his best friend, Sam, decided that they could make some money as filmmakers and started their own business. They made up flyers and advertised themselves as videographers, offering their services to film birthday parties, dance recitals, school plays, etc. Their prices were low enough that a lot of parents would have been happy to pay them to film their kids events, but Beta was on the way out and most people now had VCRs. They never made much money on the venture, but Joe did learn one important lesson from the experience...a professional is only as good as his equipment.

After high school graduation Sam went to work at his father's used car business for a few years and then moved to Los Angeles where he opened his own lot. Joe got a job delivering furniture. He spent most of his salary on cameras and equipment, and he took several night courses in photography and videography at an adult education program offered at his old high school.

When he felt confident in his equipment and in his abilities, he started advertising himself as a wedding photographer/videographer. He did a few weddings for friends and family and word soon spread that Joe was good at what he did, and that his prices were reasonable. His business grew fast. He quit his day job, rented a studio and hired his then-girlfriend, Corinne, to be his assistant. Within a year he had to hire another photographer and another videographer. He trained them on how to film a wedding Joe's way.

"Never block the guests' views if possible. Try to elevate yourself above them whenever possible....stand on a chair or on a stairway, if you can. Or stand off to the side. Just make sure you stand on the side with the best view of the bride. You gotta make the bride look good and you gotta make her the center of attention. As long as the brides are happy, bookings will keep pouring in."

Joe did all the editing himself. He made it a point to try and personalize each video with music and graphics. His clients were pleased with the final product and his business continued to grow. It wasn't long before he had saved enough money for a down payment on a home and he and Corinne began planning their own wedding. Things were going good.

And then he did something stupid.


Joe and Corinne were hanging out at her house one night watching a movie when her younger brother, Eddie, interrupted them.

"Joe, can I borrow your car for a while?" he asked.

"No!" Joe answered. Eddie was a real wild kid who was always in trouble and Joe didn't trust him with his car.

"Come on, Joe, please? I'll only be gone about a half an hour. I gotta pick up some of my stuff that I left at an ex-girlfriend's house. She's got some of my CDs and videos and I need to go get them before she changes her mind and throws them out."

"Sorry," Joe said, "but you're not taking my car."

"But I gotta do this tonight." Eddie told him, "and I can't find anybody else with a car."

"Then walk," Joe told him. "Or take a bus."

"Come on, Joe have a heart. It's cold out"

"Well, you're not taking my car, but I'll give you a ride, if you swear it will only be a half an hour."

Eddie guided Joe to the house and told him to back into the driveway and leave the car running, in case the girl's father was home and he had to leave in a hurry. Joe felt uneasy, but he followed Eddie's directions. He waited in the car while Eddie went around to the back door. He came running back to the car about 15 minutes later.

"Everything go okay?" Joe asked.

"Go!" Eddie commanded him. "Let's get outta here."

But Joe couldn't go. There were two police cars blocking their exit.

It turned out that Eddie wasn't there to pick up CDs from an ex-girlfriend. Instead, Eddie had decided to rob the home of a small-time bookie who was rumored to leave large amounts of cash around his house. He knew that the guy would be attending his mother's wake that evening and that the house would be empty. Eddie never did find the money, so he had stuffed a bag with all the small valuables that he could find. He had also set off the alarm system.

Eddie went to prison for a couple of years, but because Joe was a first-time offender, he ended up with a sentence of probation and community service. He paid his price, got on with his life and tried to put the whole incident behind him. But permanent records are permanent and the next time Joe got arrested for a crime that he had nothing to do with, his past came back to haunt him.

The other committee member's cars were already parked in The duchess's driveway when Corinne walked up to the front door. Even though they all lived in the neighborhood, Corinne was the only one who didn't drive to their meetings. She found that one of the strangest things to get used to when they first moved into the neighborhood. There were never, ever, any pedestrians on the sidewalks. When the neighborhood women wanted to take a walk, they put on their trendy 'athleisure' wear and drove to a park.

Corinne always thought of them as the 'neighborhood women' and not 'friends'. These were the women that she went to the gym with and had lunch dates with, but it was more out of boredom than friendship. She still had her friends from her old neighborhood, but she didn't see them as often as she used to. There was no more dropping by for an impromptu cup of coffee, or sitting on someone's deck after dinner and sharing a bottle of wine. Now if she wanted to get together with her old friends,it would sometimes take days of texting and emailing back and forth to make the arrangement. And often, after their plans came together and they were able to meet, Corinne felt a bit left out. Most of the conversation centered around the neighborhood where she didn't live anymore, or the local schools that her kids didn't attend anymore. She missed feeling like she was still a part of the group.

Martin, the butler, appeared at the door before Corinne had a chance to ring the doorbell.

"I'm not late, am I?" she asked him.

"No, no, Mrs. Benedetto. You're precisely on time. Precisely," he told her.

Corinne knew that the duchess hated when her guests were late. Amy had showed up fifteen minutes late for one of their meetings and the duchess had let them all know that being late was only fashionable to Americans, and that to those who were raised to believe that manners were important, it was rude. The duchess could be a pain in the ass sometimes.

"Duchess Leticia and her guests are in the solarium," Martin told her. "I'll escort you in."

"Thank you, Martin."

"My pleasure, Mrs. Benedetto. It's a beautiful day now, isn't it?"

"The weather is always beautiful here," she answered.

"Yes. So it is. It does tend to get very boring and predictable, though, for my taste."

"I suppose it could to some people. But twenty-six years of living in a climate where we had cold weather and snow every winter was enough for me. I'll take predictable over that!"

Martin ushered Corinne into the sunroom where Duchess Leticia, Nicole, Amy, Shawna and Carly were sitting around a large glass-topped table. Corinne took her place at the table and Victoria, the maid, placed a hot cup of tea in front of her.

"You may retire now, Victoria," the Duchess said to her maid.

"Thank you, ma'am," she replied with a curtsy.

"Now let's get started," the duchess said to the women seated around the table. I have the most fabulous idea for our event. I propose we have a Hawaiian luau and pig roast. Unfortunately, as I'm here without my usual staff, I'll have to rely on you ladies to make the arrangements. I wouldn't know where to start! I've always had people to do these sorts of things for me.

"Oh…and I'd like some of those exotic looking men wandering around strumming those little guitars."

"Ukuleles," Corinne said. "They're called ukuleles. And can I ask a question?"

"Well, I wasn't finished dear, but go ahead."

"I was wondering why you're here."

"What do you mean, dear?"

"What brings you to the U.S. without your staff?"

"Taxes," she answered. "I have to live outside the UK for half the year in order to avoid paying an enormous amount of tax. The travel logistics of moving the staff every couple of months is overwhelming, so they stay home and maintain the estate while I take my trips and make do with just Martin and Victoria.

"Now if there are no more questions, dear, or we can get back to our charity work."

A few minutes later Martin came back into the room.

"Excuse me," he said. "I apologize for the interruption…."

"Don't worry, Martin. Interruptions seem to be as fashionable here as tardiness. What is it?"

"You have a phone call," he answered holding out a cell phone.

"Can't you just take a message?" she asked him.

"It's um… It's 'the Boss'," he stammered and handed her the phone.

Lilibet!" she cried into the phone."What a dear, dear surprise."

Nicole's eyes lit up and she mouthed to the other woman, "It's the Queen!"

The duchess moved away from the table and went to sit in a chair in the corner where she could have a more private conversation, but Corinne noticed that she spoke loud enough for everyone to hear.

"Yes," Duchess Letitia continued, "I've seen the latest pictures. They're in all the magazines. Even over here! Such lovely children. The youngest favors you. They've changed so much since I last saw them….Did they like it?….I'm so relieved to hear that. It's so hard to find proper children's clothing in the stores here...... Yes, I did hear about his episode. Is he feeling better?....I'm so sorry to hear that....I expect to be another month, maybe two. But, if you need me....Yes, I'm sure you will....Why that's so generous of you! I graciously accept your offer....No....Yes, of course she's coming. After all, it was she who inspired me, after I visited her African school....Yes, yes she's bringing her friend, Gayle.... Goodbye and may God bless you."

The duchess sat down at the table and smiled at the women gathered around her.

"I just received a very, very generous offer from a dear friend in London. Spare no expense on the preparations for our luau, ladies. My friend has agreed to sponsor the event. That means that all the donations we receive will go directly to our building fund.

"I trust you ladies to plan a fabulous event. Just make sure to save all your receipts so I can submit them to my friend for reimbursement. We can meet here again in one week and you can fill me in on all the marvelous details. This will be one of the most successful charity events of the year, ladies. But be prepared for the inevitable paparazzi, because like it or not, your pictures will probably be in all the tabloids. And when the time comes, I'm going to invite each one of you to travel to Africa with me, all expenses paid, to help dedicate the school."

The women were all digesting the information about their impending celebrity when the duchess rose from her chair. As they all knew by now, this was the signal that the meeting was over. As she rose to leave, Corinne turned back to the duchess and said, "Can I ask another question, Duchess Leticia?"

"Of course, dear. What is it?"

"What exactly are you the Duchess of?" Corinne asked her.

"Well, that depends," she answered. "I have inherited titles from my mother, my father and my late husband, the Duke, God rest his soul. The bloodlines of the British aristocracy are very confusing to outsiders, so instead of going through all the counties and townships and hyphens, I simply refer to myself as the Duchess.

"Any other questions, dear?"

"No, I guess not." Corinne answered. "I'll see you next week."

"Yes, I suppose you will. And now Martin will see you out."

Chapter 7

Joe got up early again the next morning to have breakfast with Corinne and the kids. He knew Corinne had a busy morning and that she'd be out of the house for at least a few hours. He wanted to surprise her and start boxing up all the kitchen stuff that they could live without for a few weeks. As soon as she left the house, he grabbed a couple of boxes from the pantry and set them on the kitchen floor. He opened the first top cabinet, the one where the dishes and bowls were stored. He knew that they'd need dishes, but he had no idea how many they used each day, so he left them where they were. He opened the cabinet below and pulled out the waffle iron. They hadn't used the waffle iron in ages, but just holding it in his hands made him crave waffles. He decided that he'd ask Maria to make waffles one day this week and placed it back into the cabinet. He pulled out all the pots and pans and stared at them for a few seconds. He didn't know which ones got used on a regular basis, so he put them back. After about 45 minutes of searching the kitchen, he had only one item in the carton…the ice crusher. He decided he might make sno-cones sometime soon, so he put that back, too. He figured Corinne probably had a better idea of what they'd need, so he decided to wait until she got home and let her give him directions.

He was sitting on the couch, watching an old Clint Eastwood Western when Maria came back from walking the dog around the block.

*Geez*, he thought. *Even the dog gets around more than I do.*

Joe loved their new house, but being under house arrest was making him miss their old neighborhood. If they were still living there, he'd be able to have an occasional beer with Tony over the back fence. He used to have the guys over regularly to play cards or watch a game and order pizzas. When they first moved here they still got together regularly and talked on the phone all the time. Lately, though, it was just an occasional text or Facebook message. Joe hadn't noticed how much he missed them until he was stuck with all this time on his hands and not much to occupy it.

Fleur jumped up on Joe's lap to nap while he watched the movie. She had just settled in when he heard the doorbell ring.

"Maria," he yelled. "There's somebody at the door."

"I know, Joe. My nails are wet. Can you get it?" she yelled back.

He set the dog on the floor, mumbled a few choice expletives under his breath, and grudgingly went to answer the door. Martin, the butler from next door, stood on the landing with an envelope in his hand.

"Good day, Mr. Benedetto. Is Mrs. Benedetto home?"

"No, she's not here right now. Can I help you?"

"I have a missive for her," he answered, handing Joe the envelope.

"A what?"

"A missive... A letter from the countess."

"Countess?," Joe asked."I thought she was a duchess."

"Yes, yes, you are right. How silly of me. You see, old habits die hard, as they say. My last employer was a Countess .... Countess Hellanho-Glockenspiel. What a marvelous grande dame she was. Lived to be 103 and was healthy as a horse. Until her stroke, that is."

"Hey, Martin," Joe asked. "how would you like to come in and have a cup of coffee?"

"Oh, I'd like that very much, Mr. Benedetto. That's very kind of you. But, duty calls and I really must hurry back to the duchess. But please give my regards to Mrs. Benedetto."


Joe had barely turned around before the doorbell rang again.This time it was Will looking for him.

"Hey, Mr. B. How are you doing today?"

"Good, Will. What can I do for you?"

"We had our team meeting last night and we've come up with an idea for our television pilot project. I was hoping to run it by you, see what you think."

"Sure, I'd be glad to help. C'mon in. I'll have Maria make us some coffee. We can talk in my office.

Maria was nowhere to be found, though, so Joe grabbed a couple of Cokes and joined Will in the office.

"What's the deal with that big walled-in lot on the hill?" Will asked. "Do you use it at all?"

"No. It came with the house. I don't know the whole story, but the original owner bought two lots. He built this house on one and planned to build one for his daughter on the other lot. I guess he died before he got the chance to build it, and after his daughter inherited this house she had no use for it. By the time we bought it, the zoning laws had changed and the lot doesn't have enough frontage to build on now."

"Why does it have that huge wall around it?" Will asked.

"The last owner had a problem with teenagers partying there, so he had it walled off. The only way in now is through that solid gate behind the pool house, and that's always padlocked. The only one whoever goes up there now is your father and that's just to mow the lawn occasionally.

"Why are you so interested? Does it have something to do with your pilot?"

"Yeah. We came up with an idea and that spot would be the perfect place to film. But we need some help from you, Mr. B. Actually, we'll need a lot of help."

"I've got nothing better to do right now, Will, so I'd be happy to help. What's your idea?"

"We want to do a reality show," Will answered. "Kind of like Survivor, but not quite as intense. We'll get eight campers, four females and four males, and bring them in with just the bare essentials. We'll have rotating shifts of two cameramen at a time during daylight hours. We'll put some night-vision cameras in some of the trees and in the tent. And we'll have body mics on the campers."

"I don't know if I want a bunch of strangers living in my backyard, Will."

"You won't even be able to see them, though, Mr. B. And they'll have no idea where they are. We gotta keep the location a secret, or people might try to bust in."

"How are you going to manage that?"

"Oh, we got a great plan. Annie, our sound expert came up with this one: We rent a van or a limo and pick the contestants up at a prearranged time and place. We drive north for about an hour. Then we make them put blindfolds on and we turn around and drive back.They think they're two hours north of LA, but they're really right here in your backyard."

"Then what?" Joe asked.

"We have them set up a camp. Put up a tent, dig a fire pit.

"What are we going to feed them?" Joe asked.

"We'll give them a sack of rice and maybe some protein bars. And we'll have competitions each day where they can win some real food."

"What about a bathroom?"

"We'll rent a couple of 'porta potties'."

"What about running water? How are they going to wash and take showers?"

"They're not going to be taking showers. We'll turn the sprinkler system on every day for about five minutes. They'll have to collect their drinking and cooking water from there."

"So they're going to be hungry, thirsty and dirty? It sounds like hell."

"That's the point, Mr. B. It's supposed to be hard. They'll also have to win competitions to stay in the game."

"Where are you going to find willing campers? Why would anyone agree to this?"

"Are you kidding, Mr. B? There are thousands of people trying to get on reality shows. We're limited on who we can pick, though, because we're not offering airfare or travel expenses. But we will have to have some kind of cash prize for the winner.

"How are you going to find these people?" Joe asked.

"Were going to set up a website where applicants can send their audition tapes.Then we'll flood social media with links."

"And how are you going to pay for all of this?"

"That's another thing I wanted to talk to you about. We need some front money, but we'll have no problem paying you back. The show will pay for itself and then some. We'll set up live feeds on the website and charge people $10 a week to watch. I mean, even if we only get 10,000 people to sign up, do you know how much money that is? And since we're not allowed to make any money from the project, all the profit will go to you.

"I promise you, you'll make money, Mr. B. Also, we could use your help with production. We're going to have to post highlight reels on the website each week so that people who join later can catch up. We'll edit those highlight tapes down to a one-hour pilot, and the finished product will be our project."

"I don't know, Will…"

"Come on, Mr. B. It'll be fun *and* profitable. And, it'll give you something to do for a month."

"Is it legal?" Joe asked.

"Why wouldn't it be?" Will answered. "It's your yard. I don't know of any law that says you can't have people camp in your backyard. Besides, your name won't be connected with it.My girlfriend's a business major and she can set up a DBA or LLC or whatever you call it. And she'll set up accounts with the credit card companies.

"Would it be okay if we set up our control room in one of your garages?" Will asked.

"There's an empty apartment over that garage where I store my equipment, Will. You can use that. It'll be more comfortable and more private."

"Thanks, Mr. B."

"I hope I don't regret this, Will."

"You won't, Mr. B., it's going to be epic!

Joe wasn't convinced that it would be 'epic', but he had to admit that he was excited about the project.


Joe was on his fourth cup of coffee and second Clint Eastwood movie when Corinne returned.

"I tried to start packing up the kitchen," he told her, "but I didn't know where to start. If you tell me what you want packed, I'll box it all up and bring it out to the garage."

"You don't need to pack it up anymore," she told him. "I canceled the remodel."

"What? Why?" He asked.

"It's just a bad time, Joe," she told him, "with you out of work."

"I told you I had the money put away. We can afford it."

"I know, Joe, but it's just not a convenient time right now. You're going to be stuck here all day with the crew and the noise and dust. With Kara's graduation party coming up, along with  working on getting her ready for college, I've got too much on my plate right now to be dealing with a kitchen under construction. And you know how these things go… They always run behind schedule. What if they're not done by the time of the graduation party?

"And on top of all that, I'll be spending a lot of time working with the duchess on her charity event."

"Oh, that reminds me," Joe said, " there's a letter from the duchess for you on the table in the foyer."

"A letter? Why would she mail me a letter?"

"She didn't mail it," Joe told her. She sent Jeeves over to hand deliver it. Maybe it's an invite to Pippa's wedding."

"Very funny, Joe."


*My dearest Corinne,*

*Let me begin by thanking you for your kind offer to work as a volunteer on my charity planning committee. I do appreciate your generosity, but after working closely with one of the other members on an assignment list, I realized we had one too many volunteers!*

*I do hope you are still planning to attend the luau. I've enclosed an invitation along with a pledge card for your convenience. The poor little African girls will appreciate whatever size donation you're able to make.*

*Sincerely,*

*Duchess Letitia*


Corinne slammed the letter down on the table and picked up her phone.She started calling all the women on the committee.The first two went straight into voicemail. She didn't bother leaving a message. On the third try she reached Amy.

"I've been thrown off the committee," she told her.

"Really?" Amy seemed surprised.

"Yes, really. The Duchess said she doesn't need my help anymore. I don't know why she'd do that. Do you have any idea?" Karen asked.

"Maybe it's because you ask questions. She seems to think asking questions is rude."

"I only ask because I'm interested in her life. I mean, how often do you get to meet a real life duchess?"

"I know, right? I can't believe we were in the same room with someone was talking to The Queen of England! And I really can't believe that Oprah...Oprah!.. is coming to our luau. And Shawna knows somebody who knows Khloe Kardashian, and she thinks she might be able to get her to come, too."

"Which one is Khloe?" Corinne asked her.

"Boy, you really are out of touch," Amy answered. "Khloe is the tall one. The one who may, or may not, be OJ's daughter!"

"Amy," Corinne continued, " will you try to find out for me? "

"I wish!" she answered. "That's the million dollar question. 'Who is Khloe's father'?"

"No, not that," Corinne said. "I don't really care who Khloe is or who her father is. What I meant was, can you ask the duchess why she doesn't want me on her committee?"

"I would, Corinne, but you know how she feels about people who ask questions. I'll ask the other women if they know, though."

"You don't have to do that." Corinne said. "We're all meeting for lunch tomorrow, remember? I'll ask them myself."

"Oh, didn't you hear? No, I guess you wouldn't have. We're having a lunch meeting with the duchess tomorrow. She just called about a half hour ago. We'll have to reschedule our lunch date for sometime after the luau. We'll all be pretty busy until then."

Chapter 8

Corinne was less than excited when Joe told her about Will's plan.

"You mean you want to have a bunch of strangers living in our backyard for most of the summer?" she asked.

"They'll be confined to the vacant lot, Cor. You won't even be able to see them. Besides, it's only going to be for about three weeks. We'll have to keep it a secret, though."

"What about the kids, Joe? You don't think they'll notice teams of cameramen coming and going? Or 'mission control' or whatever you call them going in and out of the apartment?"

"We'll have to swear them to secrecy. At least until the show is over."

"I'm not sure I like the idea," she told him.

"You don't have anything to worry about, Corinne. It's not going to affect you at all. Plus it will give me something to do. And Will promises that we'll be making money off the feeds."

"I thought you said we had enough money?"

"We can always use more."

"Is it legal?" Corinne asked.

"Why wouldn't it be? It's our yard. We can let friends camp In our yard, if we want."

"They're not our friends, Joe."

"You know what I mean."

"Kara's graduation party is June 26th. They won't be here then, will they?"

"No. The plan is to have them here July 1st."

"Okay, I guess...."


Corinne was annoyed after the neighborhood women cut her out of the group, but unlike her husband, she didn't sit around feeling sorry for herself. Instead, she got busy planning Kara's party. She decided against inviting any of her current neighbors, but she did call most of her old neighbors and invited them. She also managed to make a couple of lunch dates during the calls. Then she and Maria went to work cleaning the house from top to bottom. There were relatives flying in from New Jersey for the graduation, and some of them would be staying at the house. She made hotel reservations for the rest of them.


Corinne's parents arrived on the next Wednesday, a day before everyone else was due. The graduation ceremony was on Friday night and the party was scheduled for Saturday. Corinne had asked her parents to come early, so that her mother could help with the last minute details. Joe was expected to entertain his father-in-law, which was fine with him. It was something he would have avoided under normal circumstances by claiming to have too much work to do, but now he was so bored that he was actually looking forward to his visit. Corinne's parents would be staying in the house while Joe's parents would be staying in the studio apartment. The rest of their extended family would be at a nearby hotel.

On Friday night, Maria prepared a Mexican feast for the whole brood and immediately after dinner everyone, except for Joe, left for the ceremony. After they were gone, he changed into his bathrobe, made himself a big bowl of popcorn and curled up on the couch with Fleur. He watched a poker tournament on television until he fell asleep while waiting for them to return.

Kara's graduation party was a great success. The caterers kept the food coming and the bartenders kept the drinks flowing. There was bocce ball and lawn darts for the adults, pony rides and a bouncy house for the kids, and swimmers in the pool all day. There was only one minor problem, but Joe wasn't about to let it spoil his day.

The party was just getting started and Joe was standing on the front steps greeting their guests, when he spotted Martin walking up the driveway.

"We have a small problem, Mr. Benedetto and the duchess is quite concerned," Martin told him. "Some of your guest are parking on the road in front of her property."

"So? She doesn't own the road. Besides, she can't even see the road from her house. I don't understand how that's a problem for her," Joe told him.

"It's a matter of privacy. Some of your guests are actually using her yard as a shortcut. She insists they stop."

"How neighborly. Listen, you tell the duchess that if it bothers her so much, she should call the police."

"Oh, no, Mr. Benedetto. We wouldn't want to involve the authorities, due to the publicity that might ensue. The duchess treasures her privacy."

"Good, because I don't want to call the cops, either. But if I see you trespassing on my property one more time today, I will."

"And shall I tell the duchess that you refused her request?"

"Yeah. And if she has a problem with that, you can tell her to kiss my ass."

The relatives all departed on Monday and the next day Will and his crew arrived to begin setting up for the show. They immediately accepted Joe's offer to help, and he went right to work. His ankle monitor wouldn't allow him to go as far as the campground, so he sat at a screen and gave the crew directions while they tested angles for the night cameras placed in the trees. He also helped them test the sound equipment and hand cameras. They'd have to wait to place the cameras in the tent until after the campers had finished setting it up.

There would be live camera operators filming during the daylight hours. After that, the night vision cameras would kick in, while one or more of the crew monitored them from the control room. After Will explained the set-up to Joe, he showed him the Camp Limbo website on his laptop.

"What do you think, Mr. B?" Will asked him.

Joe read the writing on the home page:

## WELCOME TO CAMP LIMBO
### NOT QUITE HEAVEN
### NOT QUITE HELL

"Did you have any trouble finding the eight campers?" Joe asked him.

"Not at all," Will told him. "in fact, we had almost 600 applicants."

"You're kidding!" Joe exclaimed.

Joe went back to checking the website. He was impressed at how professional it looked. There was even a message board where viewers could talk with each other about the show. Joe was shocked to see how many people were already using it. The last page Joe visited was the page where you signed up to pay for the live feeds.

"Anybody sign up yet?" he asked Will.

"Are you kidding, Mr. B? We've already sold the feeds to over 5000 subscribers!"

"Wow! That's quite a bit of money." Joe said.

"I told you you'd make your money back and more. And, we figure more will sign up after the show starts and word spreads."

"And you're sure this is all legal?" Joe asked.

"I don't know why it wouldn't be," he answered.

# PART THREE

# THE HAPPY
# CAMPERS

# Chapter 9

Nan was trying to find a polite way to leave her table of guests and put an end to a boring evening, when she spotted Jim Allen, her state assemblyman, across the room. He was talking to a man she didn't know, but thought she might like to. He was tall, but not too tall… maybe 6'2' or 6'3'. He was young, but not too young… maybe early forties. And he wore his tux well. It was a classic style, not too trendy, and looked to be a few years old.To Nan, that was a good sign. It meant that he probably owned, rather than rented, it. She mumbled something to her guests and excused herself from the table.

She was disappointed in the evening so far. She had invited a group of interesting people to share her table, but the mix wasn't working quite the way she had hoped, and she was glad to find a diversion. It wasn't that she particularly cared for Jim Allen as a person or a politician, but she had made a considerable donation to his last campaign (after she was pretty sure he would win) and she knew he wouldn't dare ignore her.

"Nan," he greeted her. "How nice to see you again."

"Oh, hello, Jim. I didn't know you were here. It's nice to see you, too." she said. "It's a nice turnout, isn't it?"

"Yes, yes it is," he answered.

"Ah, even more than we had hoped for," added the man next to him.

"I don't think I've met your friend," Nan told Jim.

"Nan, this is um...um...."

"Andrew," the man piped in. "Andrew Hayes."

" And Andrew this is Nan. Nan Hollinger," Jim continued.

"Are you connected with the benefit?" Nan asked Andrew.

"Yes," Andrew answered proudly. "I'm on the committee."

"How nice of you," she said. She gave Andrew a big smile, even though she was disappointed in his answer. 'On the committee' meant he was just a volunteer, and not a sponsor or donor.

"And are you on the committee, too?" he asked her.

"No," she said. "I'm just a donor. I bought a table for the event."

Andrew tried to remain nonchalant, but inside he was thinking *Good God. A whole table! This woman must be very, very rich.*

"Ah," he said "how generous."

"Well, I believe it's a good cause. The Literacy Foundation for Disadvantaged Youth is a great program with a very successful track record."

"Yes, it is," he answered. "And it's a cause that's very dear to me. You see, I'm an educator and introducing young readers to great works of literature is my passion."

*A teacher,* she thought. *An honorable career, if not very interesting or lucrative.*

"I'm also a writer," he added. "I've written two novels."

"Really?" Nan perked up. "Anything I might have read?" she asked. Jim Allen excused himself at that point. He'd already had this conversation once.

"No. Unfortunately, it's very difficult for an unknown writer to get a publishing deal. In fact, it's almost impossible"

"A lot of authors are self-publishing these days." Nan told him. "Have you considered going that route?"

"Ah, I've looked into it," he answered. "But it's a pretty expensive undertaking for someone on a teacher's salary. And without a publisher to promote your book, it's almost impossible to find readers."

"I'd like to read your work," she told him. "If I like it, I might be willing to invest in the publishing costs. I've sponsored a couple of up-and-coming artists. I like to invest in new talent. I could probably arrange some book signing appearances, too."

"That's so kind of you," Andrew gushed.

*No*, Nan thought to herself, *I'm motivated more by selfishness than kindness. Most of my single friends have found themselves a younger man, and I'd like one for myself.*

Andrew and Nan arranged to meet for lunch the next day. Andrew left it up to Nan to pick the restaurant, and she chose a place that Andrew had never heard of. It was the kind of establishment that didn't need to advertise. It was reservations-only, and you had to be a member of a certain social class to even possess the phone number. When the waiter handed them their menus, Andrew was disheartened to see that there were no prices listed. He knew what that meant. He ordered a salad and an ice water. Even though Nan had agreed to pick up the check, Andrew insisted. It was the least he could do. They had a nice lunch and when they parted Nan had a copy of the manuscript for his latest book, *The Cut of His Jib*, and Andrew had her phone number and a dinner date for the next weekend.

True to her promise, Nan read Andrew's book, or at least she tried to. The story was long, meandering and very hard to follow. It was the life story, from birth to death, of a fictional character named Alex. Nan assumed, correctly, that Alex was the man that Andrew aspired to be.

She couldn't tell him the truth, though, because Andrew was very sensitive and she didn't want to hurt his feelings and she also didn't want to jeopardize their relationship. Nan knew that they were going too fast, but she'd been a widow for three years now and she missed having a man around. And having an younger man around made her feel… well, maybe not younger exactly, but less old.

So she went ahead and paid to have it published. She also paid for a professional editor, a copyright, and a cover designer.

On the day that copies of his book arrived from the printer, Andrew decided to celebrate by asking Nan to marry him. He'd given the matter a lot of thought and decided that there were more pros than cons in marrying her. Unfortunately, children were out of the question. Nan was already a grandmother. But, on the other hand, he wasn't getting any younger, and if he hadn't found the woman he wanted to have children with by now, he probably never would. And Nan's money and connections could open so many doors for him. She might insist that he keep his job, but that was okay with him. She might insist on a prenup,too, but she'd probably leave him something in her will. And as long as she was alive he'd have entry into the kind of social world that he'd always dreamed of. The kind of world that his character 'Alex' lived in.

And, he might just become a wealthy widower one day.

Nan was equally pragmatic when he proposed. She had never gotten used to being single. She missed being part of a couple. Was it love? No. Would it do? Yes. She accepted his proposal.

Andrew's first two book signing appearances were pretty disappointing. He managed to sell a few books, but certainly not enough to recoup the publishing costs, and nowhere near enough to create any buzz. He was very optimistic,though, when he arrived for his third one. Nan had arranged for him to sign books at a big chain bookstore in the mall. He was delighted to see the author's table right inside the entrance, complete with a pitcher of ice water and a comfortable chair. He started arranging his books on the table when the manager stopped him.

"I'm sorry, Mr. Hayes," he told him. "This table is for Zack Bilow. "Your table is over there," he said and pointed to a corner in the back of the store next to the travel section.

Andrew was packing his books up when a young man strolled over. He had shoulder length blonde curls and a surfer's tan. He was wearing cut off jean shorts, a dirty white T-shirt and flip-flops.

"Dude, are you here to sign books?" he asked Andrew.

"Ah, yes, I am. Would you like me to sign one for you?" Andrew asked hopefully.

"Sure, why not? I'll sign one for you, too. I'm Zack, by the way."

"I'm Andrew. Andrew Hayes," he said as he shook the young man's hand.

"Why are you packing up?" Zack asked him.

"The manager told me this was your table. Mine is in the back," Andrew answered.

"No way, dude. You can sit here with me.There's plenty of room for both of us. Besides, nobody will even see you back there."

"Yo, dude," Zack yelled to the manager. "Bring my friend Andrew a chair. He's gonna hang with me."

"Ah," Andrew said. "That's very kind of you to share your space."

"No problem, bro. It's nice to have some company. I hate doing these things, but my agent insists. He says that it helps keep me on the bestseller list."

"You've written a bestseller?" Andrew asked him

"Well, between me and you… I didn't really write it. I just told some stories to a guy my agent hired. He made up the rest."

"What's the title?" Andrew asked him.

Zack held up a copy and Andrew read the cover out loud, " 'Zack The Wack Talks Smack' What's it about?"

"It's all about my life, but mostly about my life on reality TV shows. I was on Big Brother. I was the guy that threw all the girls clothes into the pool and put hot sauce in the wine bottles!"

"Why?"

"Because it's all about getting screen time. After that,I was on one of those celebrity rehab shows."

"And were they able to help you with your addiction?" Andrew asked.

"I didn't really have an addiction. It was just a gig. You know what I mean? There's nothing real about reality TV, but if you play your cards right and create a character you can milk a whole lot more than fifteen minutes out of it."

There was already a small crowd gathered in the mall outside the bookstore when the store opened for business. Andrew was amazed to see how many of Zach's fans showed up to buy signed copies of his book and to take selfies with him. Andrew was able to sell most of his books, too, because Zach kept directing people to him.

"Don't forget to check out my friend Andrew's book," he told them. "It's a real bargain… only $9.95. And you never know. His autograph might actually be worth something someday!"

They signed books for three hours, and it was the most successful signing event that Andrew had experienced so far. When it was over, Andrew had sold thirty-seven books, which was the most he had ever sold. His previous record had been three books.

"Ah," he said to Zack as they shook hands goodbye, "maybe I'll be seeing you at another signing?"

"Nah, answered Zack. "I'm done with these. I got asked to be a judge on a new cooking show. We start taping next week."

"Oh," said Andrew. So you have culinary experience, too?"

"No, but I like to eat. And the salary is sweet."

While driving home, Andrew couldn't stop thinking about the possibilities of promoting his book while appearing on a reality show. Nan probably wouldn't like the idea of him going away so soon after their marriage, but he was pretty sure he could convince her that it was a good idea. He felt confident that he had the type of personality that would work in his favor during the casting process. He sure wouldn't be a prankster, like Zack, but he was certainly witty and charming. He knew it was true because Nan told him so all the time.

Nan was tired of Andrew's constant need for reassurance. He was so insecure, that after every social engagement or get together with her friends or family, he would ask her, "Did I do all right? Was I a good host/guest/conversationalist? Nan couldn't tell him the truth - that she wished he would just sit there, keep his mouth shut and look good. So she would say "Yes, of course. You were charming and witty as usual."

His neediness was starting to get on her nerves. That and the way he was always pushing his stupid book. And the way he said "Ah" all of the time. So when he was accepted to be a camper on Camp Limbo, a new online reality show, she readily agreed. Maybe some time apart would be good for them. She even gave him her credit card to use for all the items he claimed he needed from LL Bean. He outfitted himself with the latest in safari fashions and included an Australian outback-style hat. He bought a top-of-the-line flashlight, high-power binoculars, and a Swiss Army Knife with all the accessories.

"I can't wear any jewelry at camp," he said to Nan before leaving for Camp Limbo, "so I've put my wedding ring on a chain for you to wear around your neck. That way I'll always be close to your heart."

"How sweet," she answered as she kissed him goodbye.

She was hoping that he wouldn't be one of the first to be voted off.

Chapter 10

Nikki was surprised to see Zeke's car parked in the driveway when she pulled in after work. She hoped he hadn't quit or been fired from another job. She was way too tired to fight. She had lost count of how many jobs he'd held since he dropped out of school after only one semester. He was already on his third job since their wedding, which had been a year and a half ago. Nikki had graduated from the two-year college that they had both attended, but she had to admit that receiving her degree hadn't helped her much. She was now waitressing full-time at the same restaurant she worked at part-time during her school years.The money was good, though, so she stayed.

Her mother-in-law was in the kitchen fixing dinner when she walked in, so she said a quick "hello" and then descended the stairs to the basement where she found Zeke and his friend, Wes, sitting on the couch and playing a video game.

"Hey, Babe," Zeke called to her. "Can you run upstairs and grab us a couple of beers while you're up?"

"How come you're not at work?" she asked him.

"I called in sick. Me and Wes had gotten so far into the game that we didn't want to stop."

"But you haven't accumulated any paid sick days yet."

"It's only one day, Nikki. It's not like we're going to starve."

"I thought we had agreed to start saving for a house."

"We will, eventually. What's the rush?" he asked her.

"I want us to have our own place," she told him. "You know that. I thought that's what you wanted, too."

"And we'll get our own place someday," he said. "It's not like we don't have a place to live."

"We're living in a basement, Zeke. We don't have our own kitchen. Or shower," she complained.

"Yeah. And we're not house-poor either. Think of it that way. We don't have a mortgage. We don't have utility bills. We can afford to do the things we like to do," he answered.

"You mean like play video games, drink beer and smoke weed? Because that's all the things you ever do."

"But those are the things I've <u>always</u> done. You knew that when you married me. Did you think I was going to change when we got married?" he asked her.

"Yes, I did," she answered. "I thought you'd grow up and act like a husband."

"Did you think I was going to become like your father?" he asked her.

"No, but I thought you were going to become a man," she shot back.

"Ouch," yelled Wes. "Get the ointment, because that was a burn."

"Goodbye, Wes," Nikki said.

"A few more minutes," Wes answered. "I'm almost done with this level."

"Goodbye, Wes," she said more forcefully.

"Yeah, okay," he said handing Zeke the controller."I'll catch up with you later, bro"

When Wes had left, Zeke stood up and put his arms around Nikki.

"Hey," he said, "It's just one day off from work. I'll try to pick up some overtime next week to make up for it, okay? And don't worry, we'll have our own place soon. I promise. I promise I'll be more responsible about money, too. I'll even start giving you money every week to put away, okay?"

"Yeah, I guess," she said.

"Good. Now let's go upstairs and see what's for dinner. It must be close to time to eat. I wonder what my mom's cooking tonight."

"You go," she said. "I'm not hungry. I ate at work."

After Zeke went upstairs, Nikki sat down at the computer and started searching for tiny houses. She was determined that she and Zeke would move out of her in-laws' basement sooner rather than later, and she felt a tiny house might be the only way they could afford to have their own home. She'd like to find one that had a little land, or at least a yard, but she'd settle for having one built on a trailer. It would still be their own home, even if they had to park it in her in-law's backyard.

She searched for 'tiny houses' and 'cabins' and found nothing for sale that was both affordable and close to their jobs. Sometimes cabins were listed as camps, so she searched 'camps', too. She soon realized that the search was too broad. She was about to refine her search when she noticed the link to Camp Limbo along with a blurb announcing a $50,000 prize. She clicked on the link.

Nikki showed Zeke the Camp Limbo website when he came back downstairs after dinner

"We could win $50,000, Zeke," she told him excitedly, "just for going camping for three weeks. With the money we've got saved, that would give us enough to build a tiny house."

"We've got money saved?" Zeke asked her.

"Yeah. I opened a savings account right after we got engaged. I've been putting money away every week," she told him.

"And how come I didn't know about this money?" he asked.

"Because we wouldn't have anything left if you had known about it," she answered sarcastically.

"So which one of us should apply?" Zeke asked.

"We should both apply. That'll double our chances of getting a spot," she answered.

"What about our jobs?"

"Let's face it, Zeke, neither one of us is on any kind of career path at work. We can always get new jobs when we come back, if we have to."

"Okay," he agreed. "Let's do this!

Chapter 11

Vonda sat in front of her computer studying a spreadsheet. The numbers were good, but not great. She really wanted to grow her business and add a couple more products, but she needed extra capital first.

She had applied to be on 'Shark Tank' and had gotten pretty far in the casting process before she was told that she wouldn't be featured on the show. The fragrance market was saturated, they told her. There really wasn't room for her products. She tried to explain that 'e-scentuals', her company, was different. Her fragrances were unique. Buyers were able customize them. You could have different scents for different moods, or you could create your own signature fragrance she explained to them, but it didn't help any.

'e-scentuals' sold scented body lotions and body sprays online. There was a list of scented oils that they offered, and buyers could choose up to three different oils for each product they ordered. Vonda bought the lotion, spray, and oils in bulk. She had two part-time workers who helped mix them and package them in bottles that Vonda had designed herself before they shipped them to the customers. Vonda wanted to add soaps and candles to her line, but she wasn't making enough profit to invest in more inventory.

Her twin, Ronda, sat across from her, sipping a cup of tea and tossing out ideas.

"Why don't you take a second mortgage out on your condo?" Ronda asked.

"I looked into that, but I don't have enough equity," she answered.

"Well, I know you didn't make it onto 'Shark Tank', so why don't you apply for another reality show....like Survivor or Big Brother?"

"And how is that going to help me? You only make big money if you win. I'd probably lose money by being away from the business for that long."

"But think of all the free advertising you'll get. You can have t-shirts made for you to wear on-air and you can talk about your product to a huge audience," her sister answered.

"Do you really think they're going to let me on a show in order for me to sell my own products? I'm sure their sponsors might have a problem with that," Vonda said.

"First of all," Ronda said, " you don't tell them that you own a business. And they can't stop you from wearing the shirts or talking about the company."

"I think I'll pass," Vonda told her. "It doesn't sound like a very reliable marketing technique."

Vonda was packing up orders for shipping the next morning when Ronda stopped by for a visit. While Vonda was making them some tea, Ronda sat down at the computer and pulled up the website for Camp Limbo.

"Look at this, Vonny," she said to her when she sat down. "You could do this. You'd only have to be away for about three weeks. Your staff could run things on their own for that short period of time. Plus, Jordan and I will help out."

"And what if you go into labor while I'm away?" Vonda asked her. "I'd feel horrible, if I wasn't here with you."

"Jordan will be with me. I'll be fine. If anything goes wrong, I'll make sure we get word to you somehow. You should do this."

"I don't know….."

"Look," Ronda went on, "all these shows are always looking for a sassy black girl. You just have to make an audition tape showing them you're *that* sassy black girl."

"I'm hardly the sassy type," Vonda said.

"I know that. But you were in Drama Club for three years. You know how to play a character. Remember Tania Phillips from middle school?"

"Yeah, I remember Tania. I was afraid of her."

"Everybody was afraid of Tania," Ronda said with a chuckle. "Even the boys were afraid of her.

"You've got to channel your inner Tania," she continued. "You have to copy her attitude and swagger. And never, ever admit that you're a Harvard grad," Ronda advised her.

"Keep it real, huh?" Vonda joked.

"There's nothing real about reality shows," Ronda quipped.

Ronda reached into her purse and pulled out a scarf. She wrapped it around her hair and then grabbed Vonda's phone. She turned on the video camera and began recording herself.

"Hey, Camp Limbo. My name is Vonda. Yeah, just Vonda, and I'm applying to be on your show. Now you and I both know that you ain't gonna pick me, so you might ask yourself why I'm bothering. It's because I want to represent! That's right. REPRESENT!! Now I see all those women of color that you cast on your shows. They got the straight hair from the Indian girl. They got the plastic nails from the Vietnamese girl, and they got the green eyes from Bausch and Lomb. That's the truth. But I represent a different truth. One that you'all are afraid of.

"So are you looking for Miss America? Or are you looking for reality? Because I'm as real as it gets.

"Or am I too real for you?"

Ronda handed the phone back to Vonda when she was done.

"There," she told her. "You've applied."

Chapter 12

Cassie had a big surprise to share with her parents, so she waited until they all sat down for dinner together to give them the news.

"I've managed to get the whole month of July off from work," she told them. "I had to scramble around and arrange for others to cover my shifts, but I did it!"

"That's nice, Cassie," her mother replied. "But why did you need a whole month? Do you have plans?"

"I did it so that I could go away with you and Dad," she answered. "You said that you were renting a beach house for the month. I did it so that I could come with you."

"We're renting it with two other couples, Cassie. I thought I told you it was a couples vacation."

"Well, don't either of these couples have children?" she asked.

"Yes," her mother answered. "We're going with the Millers and the Donatos. You know their kids. They're all adults now...like you. And you can hardly consider yourself a child at 32."

"That's not fair, Mom. We always go to the park for the fireworks on the fourth together. It's like a family tradition. And what am I supposed to do for a whole month while you're away?"

"I'm sure you can find a friend from work to go with you to the fireworks. And, as long as you have all this free time, why don't you go visit your sister? Raymond's going to be leaving for Afghanistan soon, and Linda will have her hands full with those three little boys. I'm sure she'd appreciate some help."

Cassie snorted. "I didn't take time off from work to be a free babysitter for Linda," she told her mother. "In fact, I get a little tired of how everybody's always worrying about Linda and helping out Linda. Nobody ever helps me with anything."

"Oh, stop it, Cassie. I'm tired of hearing your complaints. Your father and I paid for your education and financially supported you through college and grad school. We've even allowed you to live here rent-free....."

"Allowed me?" Cassie interrupted. " ALLOWED ME? This is my home, too!"

".....until you found a full-time job," her mother continued. "It's been eight years, Cassie, and you're still working part-time in the museum gift shop with no hope of promotion. I think it's time you move on to a real job and start contributing your fair share."

"But the museum is like my second home, Mom. And it's not my fault that I haven't been able to break the glass ceiling. I'm a victim. A victim of politics, nepotism and sexism.

"But, of course, you *never* see my side."


Cassie jumped out of her chair, stomped upstairs to her bedroom and slammed the door shut. She lay on her bed, pouting for a while, until she came up with an idea. She'd ask her mother to call the other couples and ask them if they would mind Cassie coming along for a week or two. She could sleep on the couch…she wouldn't be any trouble…she'd pay her own way. She couldn't imagine why anyone would have a problem with that. She gave herself a few minutes to calm down and practice what she'd say to her parents before she left her bedroom to return to the dining room. She was almost to the bottom of the stairs when she heard her father say, "Maybe we should buy the plot next to ours while it's still available. Just in case she ends up alone."

Cassie immediately returned to her bedroom and sat down at her desk. *I'll show my parents*, she said to herself. *I'll find something to do in July that will make their stupid beach vacation look boring by comparison.* Then she opened her laptop and started searching.

Chapter 13

Justin was packing up the belongings in his dorm room when his phone began ringing. He glanced at the caller ID and saw that it was his parent's phone number. He decided to ignore the call. He knew why they were calling and he was dreading the inevitable conversation. He'd had his last final the week before, but he had waited till the deadline to leave the dorm before he made his way home. He knew he'd have to face them sooner or later, but he'd tell them that he was behind the wheel when the phone rang, in order to delay the confrontation. He had a two and a half hour drive home, and he hoped to come up with a plausible excuse during the ride.

He was going to miss school. Not school really, but campus life. He'd miss living in the dorm, going to local bars where underage drinking was allowed, playing beer pong with the guys and the freedom that came with being away from home. He'd especially miss the freedom.

He felt sad as he pulled out of the campus parking lot for the last time and began the long drive home. He drove slower than usual. He was in no rush to get home.

When he arrived home, he parked in the driveway and as he was getting out of the car, he could see his mother coming toward him waving a sheet of paper.

"Hi, Mom," he said with as much cheer as he could muster.

"We need to talk, Justin," she said.

"Yeah, I know, Mom," he told her. "Just let me unpack my car first."

"I've got your marks, Justin," she said angrily.

"I know. Can you help me carry some of my stuff in?"

"YOU FLUNKED OUT! How did this happen?" she asked him.

Justin stood in front of her, staring at the ground, not saying a word.

"I asked you how this happened, Justin. You heard me. Now answer me," she demanded.

"Yeah, I heard you. Geez...I think the neighbors heard you. We can talk about it when we get inside," he answered.

"Then get inside. NOW!!"


"How could you do so poorly?" she asked him as soon as they entered the house. "You didn't even show up for one of your exams."

"It wouldn't have mattered much, if I did take it," he told her. "I had such a low average in the class that even if I had aced the final I still couldn't have passed the course.

"Does Dad know?"

"Of course he knows. I called him as soon as I found out," she answered.

He's going to kill me isn't he?"

"No, he's not going to kill you. But he is putting you to work. You've wasted two years. Two years at school and you've accomplished nothing. You're going to pay us back at least some of your tuition, Justin. Starting Monday you'll be working for your father. Full time," she said.

"I can't do kitchen and bathroom remodeling," he told her. "It's not my thing."

"It's your thing now," she told him.

"I've got a plan, though. I'm going to try to get my old high school bandmates together. We were pretty good. We can probably line up a few gigs and make some money."

"Fine," his mother replied, " but you'll still be working for your father during the day."

"I can't do both, Mom," he told her. "If I want to make money playing guitar, I have to keep my hands in good shape. Construction work is too tough on the hands."

'It's already settled, Justin. Unless you can find a way to pay your dad and I back in the meantime, you'll be installing drywall on Monday morning."

Chapter 14

Kyle was taking his time getting ready for his date with Christie. He couldn't decide if he was looking forward to the date or dreading it. Christie was the prettiest and sweetest girl he'd ever met, and he felt lucky to have her for a girlfriend. But he was afraid that she might not feel the same way after what had happened the night before.

It had started like a typical Friday night date. They met Craig and Julie at the bowling alley and shared a pizza and a pitcher of soda while they bowled. Kyle thought Christie looked beautiful as always, but that maybe her skirt was a little too short for bowling. Every time she bent forward to throw her ball, he got a view that made his heart rate soar. He knew Christie was a sweet, naïve girl and he didn't want to embarrass her, so he didn't mention it. But he couldn't stop looking.

After they left the bowling alley Kyle drove Christie home. He parked in the driveway where they sat talking in his car for a while. Talking led to kissing and the next thing he knew, his hands were on her thighs and inching up Christie's leg. He felt her flinch when he reached her underwear and he realized he'd gone too far. Before either of them had a chance to react any further Christie's parents car pulled in the driveway and parked next to them. Christie gave Kyle a quick peck on the cheek before she got of the car and went to join her parents.

Kyle hadn't talked to Christie since he'd said goodnight to her in her parent's driveway. He received a couple of texts from her earlier that day: 'what time 2night' and 'c u then'. Kyle had responded, but they'd had no real conversation. He thought it might be a good idea to pray before he left for their date, so he knelt down at his altar to ask for forgiveness and strength. His altar was really just an old coffee table he had brought in from the garage and sat at the foot of his bed. He had covered it with a black cloth cut from the cape his mom had made for him years ago for a school play. He had placed two framed pictures of Jesus, his Bible, a plastic crucifix and a handful of stones with inspirational phrases painted on them. After a five-minute prayer session, in which he asked for help in controlling himself, he went to pick up Christie.

She was waiting on her front steps when he pulled into the driveway. She was wearing an even shorter skirt than the one she had on the night before, along with a tank top that showed her bra straps. Jesus was testing him.

"What do you feel like doing tonight?" he asked her when she got in the car. "I was thinking maybe a movie or mini-golf."

"Let's go someplace where we can be alone," she answered. "We really need to talk, Kyle."

*Uh-oh*, he thought. *Here it comes.* Kyle knew that when a girl said "We need to talk" that it usually meant that bad news was coming.

"We can talk while I drive," he said.

"Let's go find a secluded spot in the sandpit instead," she answered.

She was uncharacteristically quiet on the drive. Christie was usually talkative and outgoing. He was getting more and more worried as he drove. When they reached the sandpit, Christie told him to park at the far end, next to a large bulldozer where the car couldn't be seen by anyone driving by.

Kyle pulled in and killed the engine. Christie unbuckled her seatbelt, put her arms around him and gave him a passionate kiss.

"Let's get in the back seat," she said. "Let's finish what we started last night."

"No, Christie. We shouldn't. It wouldn't be right. Besides I love you and I have way too much respect for you to do this."

"And I appreciate that, Kyle. You're the only guy I've ever dated that didn't want sex all the time and I love that about you.

But I think it's time we took our relationship to the next level. Don't you?" she asked hopefully.

"I can't, Christie. I promised that I'd wait until marriage."

"Promised who?" she asked.

"Jesus! And my mother," he told her.

"Do you really think that Jesus cares if two people show their love for one another? And your mother would understand, Kyle. She's a grown woman. After all, she's had three babies. She's done it herself."

"I can't believe you're talking about my mother like that. My mother!" Kyle cried.

"Do you really love me, Kyle?" she asked him.

"Of course, Christie. You know I do." he answered.

"Then prove it," she challenged him.

"I will prove it. I'll marry you as soon as we can afford our own place. But I think we should remain virgins until our wedding night," he told her.

"Kyle, I'm only 19! I'm not ready to get married. And, I never said I was a virgin."

Kyle's head was spinning. He had just assumed that Christie was 'pure', and that she wanted to marry him as much as he wanted to marry her.

"I think you should take me home now, Kyle," she told him. "And you should go home and think about what I said. I'll see you at church tomorrow and you can let me know your decision then. Do you want to take our relationship to the next step or break up?" she asked.

"In church?? You want to talk about sex at church!" In front of God? And Jesus? I'm not sure if I even know who you are anymore, Christie," he told her.


When Kyle returned home he went straight to his altar and knelt down to pray. Reagan, the family cat, kept trying to play with his inspirational stones, so Kyle picked him up and set him on the desk chair. Reagan jumped up on the desk, walked across Kyle's computer keyboard and brought the screen out of sleep mode. Kyle's Facebook page popped up. Reagan then jumped back onto the 'altar' and started batting the stones around. Kyle couldn't concentrate on his prayer with all the distractions. He went to grab Reagan and shoo him into the hall when the post on the screen caught his eye:

## WELCOME TO CAMP LIMBO

### NOT QUITE HEAVEN.....NOT QUITE HELL

It was a sign. His prayers had been answered.

# Chapter 15

Edna May pulled up to the designated meeting spot and checked her watch. She was about a half hour early, so she decided to drive around the block a few times, just to kill some time. She didn't think that she would feel comfortable waiting alone in the parking garage.

She noticed that her gas tank was almost empty, so after her fourth ride around the block, she pulled into the garage. She told the parking attendant who she was there to meet and he directed her to the second floor, slot number 24. It was hot inside the garage, and even hotter in the car, but she felt safer inside. She didn't have enough gas in the tank to keep the engine running, and even if she did, it wouldn't help anyway. The air conditioner wasn't working. She felt too exposed with the windows open, so she sat in the hot car, with the doors locked, and waited. She was having second thoughts concerning what she was about to do, and she wondered if she should just leave and forget the whole thing. *But where would I go?* she asked herself. *I have a car that barely runs, no home, no real job and $241.86 in the bank. What do I have to lose?*

But then she thought *What if the whole thing is a scam... or a white slavery ring? And even if it's not, chances are I'll end up back here with nothing but an empty gas tank.*

She was still trying to come to a decision ten minutes later, when a car pulled into the slot next to hers. A girl not much older than Edna May exited and walked over to Edna May's car. She tapped on the window and motioned for Edna May to follow her. She was wearing a khaki shirt with a patch over the pocket that read: 'Camp Limbo Transportation'.

Edna May's instinct was to trust the girl, so she decided to forget about her problems for a while and go camping.

# PART FOUR

# CAMP LIMBO

Chapter 16


The crew realized that the original transportation plan needed some tweaking. They all agreed that the campers shouldn't meet each other until the cameras started rolling. That meant that they needed seven drivers, because Nikki and Zeke could ride together. But because there were only eight students on the crew, and Will needed to be at the campsite when the campers arrived, Joe was enlisted to man the control room until the drivers returned. Since Will was the only crewmember who would appear on camera, it was necessary to keep his identity secret, otherwise some viewers might recognize him and figure out where Camp Limbo was located. To avoid that happening, Will wore a mask and spoke with a Mexican accent.

Each driver picked up their passenger at a different slot in the garage. From there they formed a convoy to Joe's house, normally a fifteen-minute drive. Their route took them about 1 1/2 hours. They assumed, correctly, that their blindfolded passengers would believe that they were traveling for over two hours. They had covered the clock and mileage meters with duct tape, just to be on the safe side.

The campers stood in a line while the crew attached their mics. When that was done, the campers were instructed to sit on the ground while two members picked up their cameras and the rest ran down to the control center. There would be two cameramen at the site during daylight hours and at least one person monitoring the control center at all times. There was never a shortage of crew members, because the crew ended up practically living in the tiny studio apartment. It was cramped, but they were so engrossed in the project that they didn't seem to notice or care. To them, it was like being on a professional production crew, something that every one of them hoped to do someday. Joe was amused that eight college students, six guys and two girls, could live together in a space that Corinne had deemed too small for a toddler and his 4'11" mother.

## "AND WE'RE LIVE!"

Joe and the crew watched from the studio where several monitors were set up. One camera was pointed at Will, who was wearing a Camp Limbo t-shirt and a Phantom of the Opera-type mask. The other cameraman was filming the campers, still blindfolded, sitting on the ground in front of Will.

"You may now remove your blindfolds," Will told them.

The campers pulled off their blindfolds and looked around. If anyone was surprised to see a masked man standing in front of them, they didn't show it. The only noticeable reaction was from Justin. His eyes grew wide and his mouth dropped open when he spotted Edna May. Joe was having a similar reaction in the control room.

"Welcome to Camp Limbo," Will continued. "My name is Guillermo, and I'll be your camp director. Camp Limbo is located on a private campsite surrounded by ten-foot walls. The only way in or out is through that solid wooden gate, which will remain locked at all times. Any camper that is caught trying to leave will have their camping permit immediately and permanently revoked.

"There are a pair of porta-potties in the far left corner. One for men and one for women. Those are the only spots in camp without cameras or microphones. There are cameras hidden in several trees and there will be cameras and microphones in your tent. You may only remove your mics in the tent or in the porta-pottie.

"Where's the shower?" Cassie asked.

"There is no shower. There is, however, an underground sprinkler system. Each day the sprinkler will be turned on for five minutes. During that time you must use the buckets provided for each of you to collect your water for the day. That will be all the water you'll have for drinking, cooking and washing.

"We've also provided you with a barrel of rice and a crate filled with protein bars in that storage locker over there and next to that, there's a barrel to store your water in," Will/Guillermo told them as he pointed in the direction of the locker. There are only enough bars for each camper to have one per day. Make sure you ration your rice wisely, because the barrel will not be refilled.

"You'll have a competition each day where the winner be able to earn extra food. On every third day, the two campers who perform the worst in the competition will be in danger of losing their camping permits. There will be a campfire meeting on the following day where the other campers will vote to decide which one of them will have their permit revoked. When there are three campers left, the internet audience will have twenty-four hours to vote for the winner. The winner will receive $50,000.

"If you are unfortunate enough to lose your permit, you will be driven to The Bradley Motor Inn, where you'll have a pre-paid reservation to stay in one of their clean and spacious rooms for one night. You'll also be given $100 in cash, which you may choose to spend in one of The Bradley Inn's dining spots. There's The Bradley Coffee Shop, which serves breakfast all day, along with a selection of light meals. They also have The Bradley Deli where the menu includes salads, sandwiches and burgers. Or you may choose to eat in the fine dining room of The Bradley Grill. They also offer room service. After you check out on the next morning, The Bradley Inn Shuttle Service will deliver you to your car.

"Are you ready for your first competition?" He asked.

Edna May raised her hand "Mr. Guillermo..." she started.

"You don't have to raise your hand. And it's just Guillermo." he told her.

"Okay, Guillermo. I was just wondering if we could have one of those protein bars before we start the competition. I'm pretty hungry."

Guillermo took eight  bars out of the crate in the storage locker and handed them to the campers.

"I'll explain the rules while you eat," he told them. "This will be your first team challenge. I have a bag with eight Scrabble tiles inside: four 'T's  and four 'F's. You'll each pick a tile. Those who pick 'T's will be tasked with putting up the tent. You must use the area that's been staked out for you. The sprinklers in that area have been deactivated. The campers who picked 'F's will have to dig a fire pit and line it with the stones that are piled here to the left of the tent. You'll also find two shovels there. We've drawn a chalk outline to give you an idea of how wide your hole must be. The first team to finish their assignment wins the reward. The winning team will receive four sleeping bags along with all the fixings to make s'mores.

"Any questions?"

None of the campers had any questions, so Will announced, "The competition starts….Now!"

Edna May, Nikki, Cassie and Andrew all picked 'F's, while Vonda, Kyle, Jason and Zeke each picked 'T's. Vonda was disappointed in both her task and her team. While digging a fire pit was more physically taxing, she thought, it was a more straight forward, and much simpler task, than trying to erect a huge tent with the redneck and two 'bros' she was stuck with.

Nikki stepped up to lead the other team. Her first decision was that they should move the fire pit to a different location.

"The smoke's going to blow right into the tent if we leave it where it is," she told her team. "I've been camping all my life, and I know how to set up a campsite."

"But maybe they put it here for a reason," Edna May suggested. "I think we should dig right here. The tent will probably have a flap that we can close."

"How often do you go camping?" Nikki asked.

"I've never been camping," she answered," but it seems to me that they want us to put it here. That's why there's an outline."

"I know what I'm doing," Nikki told her. "The outline is just to give us an idea of the size. I mean, the guy pretty much said as much. Do you want to help with this or do you want to stand here and argue?" she asked.

Edna May and Andrew began digging in the spot designated by Nikki, while Nikki and Cassie carried the rocks to the new fire pit location. Work on the tent wasn't progressing very fast, either. The guys had laid out all the pieces on the ground, but couldn't seem to figure out how to put it together.

"Did any of you check inside the box to see if the instructions were included?" Vonda asked her teammates.

"Yeah," Justin answered. "They're no help, though, because they're in Chinese. I put them back in the box."

Vonda pulled the instruction sheet out of the box and took a look at it.

"There are pictures," she told them.

"Yeah, but all the writing is in Chinese," Justin said."

When Vonda was thirteen she decided that she wanted to be an architect, like her mother, so her parents sent her to a camp that had an architecture program. She liked it so much that she went back the next two summers in a row. Her career choices had changed many times since then, but she still remembered a lot of what she had learned at camp. She could read simple blueprints, so she figured she could read a how-to diagram for erecting a tent.

"You have to put the floor cloth down before you put the poles up," she told her teammates.

"Wow," Zeke said. "You can read Chinese?"

She ignored his question.

With Vonda giving directions, the tent began taking shape. She looked over at the firepit team and was disappointed when she saw the progress they had made.

And then the sprinklers came on.

"Grab your buckets and go," called Will/Guillermo. "You only have five minutes to collect water," he reminded them.

Everyone dropped what they were doing and ran for the buckets. The water from the sprinklers spray was only about knee-high, but the ground became slippery after a minute or two and there was a lot of slipping and falling. When the five minutes were over, the campers were wet and muddy and had only filled their water barrel about half way.

The campers returned to the competition only to find out that the fire pit was ruined. They had placed it too close to the sprinklers. There was a small puddle in the bottom and the piles of dirt they had excavated had turned to mud and were beginning to slide back into the hole. They'd have to go back to the original location and begin all over again. Team Tent won the first competition.

Everyone, with the exception of Nikki, pitched in to help finish the firepit. Nikki claimed that she had a headache and needed to lay down on the floor of the tent for a while. She rejoined the group only after they had finished the pit, had a fire going and Edna May had begun cooking the rice.

"Ah," said Andrew, when they were all sitting around the firepit waiting to eat, "smell that clean air. You can tell we're far from a major city just by the way the air smells."

"It doesn't smell different than any other air to me," Vonda replied.

"I think it smells different," he told her. "It smells......*earthy*....With a floral hint."

"I think that's me you're smelling," she answered.

Edna May sat down beside Vonda while she waited for the rice to finish.

"You're right," she said to Vonda. "I think it is you. What are you wearing that smells so nice?"

"It's my signature scent," Vonda answered. "I order online from e-scentuals.com. They sell body creams and sprays and they custom mix them to your taste. Mine is two parts musk and one part tea rose."

"It smells beautiful," Edna May told her.

119

"It's really inexpensive, too," Vonda added. "And free shipping on orders over $50."

"That's pretty cool having your own signature scent." Edna May said. "And by the way, my name is Edna May."

"No, it's not," cried Justin."I know who you are…you're Misty Manx! I've seen all of your movies. I even had your poster on my dorm room ceiling. Wow! My buddies are going to be soooo jealous when they see me camping with Misty Manx!"

"Ah" said Andrew. "So you're a thespian?"

Cassie snorted.

"No," answered Edna May. "I just played one in the movies. And my name really is Edna May. And I don't…..*act* anymore."

"So tell us about yourself," Edna May said to Andrew, in order to try and change the subject.

"My name is Andrew and I'm forty-one years old. I like to call myself a man of words. I love literature and I've spent my life trying to stir up that same kind of passion for the written word in the younger generation."

"And I thought you were Crocodile Dundee," Justin joked. "You know..because of the hat."

Zeke and Nikki laughed, while Cassie offered her opinion.

"I like the hat," she said.

"And do you have a big knife, too?" Zeke asked.

"Yes," Andrew answered. "I do. A Swiss Army Knife."

Justin, Zeke and Nikki all laughed, and Cassie said, "I think bringing it was a smart idea. I'll bet it'll come in handy."

"So, Wordman," said Vonda, "you're like what? A high school English teacher or something?"

"Ah, middle school, actually. But I'm also a writer," he answered.

"How interesting," Cassie said. " A writer! And what type of writing do you do?"

"Well, I've written two novels so far and I just recently published one. I've brought a couple of copies with me, in case anyone would like to read it."

"I"ll give it a try," Vonda offered.

"Oh… I'd love to read it," Cassie piped in."I have such respect for writers, or any kind of artist actually. In fact, I work in a museum. Oh, and my name is Cassie and I'm twenty-eight."

*Twenty-eight, my ass* Vonda thought to herself.

"Working in a museum must be pretty interesting," commented Edna May. "What kind of stuff do you do?"

"Well, I only work part time in the gift shop right now, but to be honest, I practically run the place." she answered.

"How do you support yourself?" Vonda asked. "Are you married?"

"No, I'm single," Cassie told her. She looked at Andrew to see if he had any reaction to her availability. " I share a home with my parents, so my expenses are pretty low. It's difficult to find a job in my field. I'm at a disadvantage, too, because I'm a woman and I'm over-educated. Some men find that threatening."

"What a cross to bear," Vonda said.

"I know." Cassie replied. "Right? And what do you do…?"

"Vonda. My name is Vonda, and I'm twenty-five. I do a little of this and a little of that. Whatever it takes to pay the rent. Know what I mean?"

Cassie was just about to answer, *No, I don't know what you mean* when Justin spoke up. "My name is Justin, and I just turned twenty-one. I just finished my second year of college and I decided to apply for Camp Limbo, because it was either that or work for my father all summer."

"I'm Nikki," Nikki told the group, " and this is my husband, Zeke. We're both twenty-two and we applied because we're trying to save up to buy a tiny house."

"Dude, my friend has one of them," Justin told them.

Nikki's ears perked up. She never got tired of talking about tiny houses.

"Is it a foundation build or is it on a trailer?" she asked.

"There's no trailer, so I guess it's a foundation. It's on a slab in his parent's backyard," Justin answered.

"Did he have it built, or did he build it himself?" Nikki asked.

"His father bought it at Home Depot," Justin told her.

"They sell tiny houses at Home Depot?" Zeke asked.

"Well, it's really a shed, but his mom fixed it up real nice for him. He's got a sofa bed and a flatscreen and even a little refrigerator and microwave.."

"We could do that, Nikki," Zeke said."I'll bet it costs a lot less than a tiny house."

"Does it have a bathroom?" Nikki asked Justin.

"No, there's no plumbing. But it's only about twenty feet from his parents backdoor. Plus, he's a guy…"

"That wouldn't work for us," she told Zeke. "I need a real bathroom."

"You're such a princess," he told her.


Edna May checked the rice and decided it was ready. She portioned it out into the bowls and spoons that had been supplied for them. She noticed that Kyle bowed his head and said a prayer before he ate, and she realized that he hadn't been given a turn to introduce himself. When he raised his head, she caught his eye and asked him his name.

"I'm Kyle," he answered. "I'm twenty-one years old and I'm a prayer warrior.

Nikki rolled her eyes.

Cassie snorted.

After they had finished their meal, Edna May collected the bowls. She cleaned them, along with the cooking pot, as best she could while using as little water as possible. Andrew slipped into the tent and came out a few minutes later carrying his flashlight and Swiss Army Knife.

"I'm going to check the perimeter," he told the other campers.

"Dude," said Justin, " you can see the perimeter from here. There's a big stone wall behind the trees that goes all around the campsite."

"Yes I know," Andrew told him. "I want to look around and see if I can find anything that might be useful to us...like edible plants or roots"

"So, are you a botanist, too, Wordman?" Vonda asked.

"Ah, no," he answered, "but I did a lot of research on how to survive in the wild before I came here, just in case."

"I ain't eating no weeds," Vonda told him.

"Let's hope it doesn't come to that," Andrew said. "But you never know."

"No, I **do** know that I'm not eating weeds. And I also know that they're not going to let us starve to death, Wordman," Vonda said.

"And neither am I," Andrew answered.

Alex, the hero of Andrew's book *The Cut of His Jib*, was a natural leader and Andrew decided to pattern himself after Alex during his time at Camp Limbo. He didn't seem to realize that he was recreating himself in the image of a character that he had created. He felt that Alex would assume the role of leader in a group situation, and so Andrew would assume the role of leader at Camp Limbo. As he strolled off to search the campsite, Cassie joined him. He had his first follower.

The eight campers sat around the campfire while four of them devoured their s'mores and the other four jealously watched them.

"I think it's rather rude that you're sitting here and eating in front of the rest of us," Nikki told them.

"They won them fair and square," Edna May said. "And besides, you need the campfire to make s'mores."

"Yeah, but they could make their stupid s'mores and then walk away to eat them."

"Or you could walk away," Zeke suggested.

Nikki ignored him.

Cassie turned to Andrew and said, "I see you're a fan of Barbara Bush."

"Barbara Bush?" he asked her. "What gave you that idea?"

"I saw her picture propped up on your backpack," she answered.

"That's not Barbara Bush," he said. "That's my Nan. She's the proverbial woman behind the man. She's the one who encouraged me to publish my book. I couldn't have done it without her."

"How sweet!" Cassie replied.

All the campers were tired from the long day, and they soon all decided to go to bed for the night. When Nikki entered the tent, she started to get into Zeke's sleeping bag.

"Whoa," he said. "Do you really want to do it with all these people around?"

"Of course not," she answered. "I'm tired and I just want to get some sleep."

"Sorry, babe, but I won the sleeping bag and there isn't really room in it for two."

"But I'm your wife," she protested.

"I know, and I love you. But I gotta get some sleep. Good night, loser."

"You can be a real asshole sometimes," she said.

"Misty," yelled Justin. "I'll share my sleeping bag with *you*."

"It's Edna May," she answered. "And no, thank you."

"C'mon, Misty. You can make all of my fantasies come true just by sliding in here with me. Please?"

"No, thank you," she said again.

"Misty, I'll make it worth your while. I promise," he continued.

"SHE TOLD YOU HER NAME IS EDNA MAY, AND SHE TOLD YOU 'NO THANK YOU'. SO ZIP IT, OR ELSE," Vonda yelled.

"She'll always be Misty Manx to me," Justin answered. "And are you trying to threaten me? Because I'm not scared of you, Vonda."

"Well then your mama must have dropped you on your head when you were a baby and knocked all the common sense out. Now shut up and let the rest of us get some sleep."

"Who's gonna make me?" he taunted.

"I might," answered Kyle.

Justin's opinion was that Kyle was just a dumb farm boy. But he was a *big*, dumb farm boy, so Justin decided to leave Misty alone. For now.

Chapter 17

Edna May was the first camper to wake up on their first morning at Camp Limbo. She already had the fire going and was boiling water for the rice when the crew arrived at 6 AM. She was sitting on the ground with a bucket beside her and it was full of things that she had collected – sticks, twigs, weeds and vines. She was sorting them into piles. By the time the other campers emerged from the tent, the rice was ready and she had fashioned an item that vaguely resembled a broom.

"The floor of the tent is getting pretty gritty already," she explained.

She gave each of the campers a cup with just enough water inside to brush their teeth. They'd have to sacrifice washing up in order to have enough drinking water, but Edna May had brought a container of wet wipes and she handed two to each camper. After they had cleaned themselves as best as they could she passed everyone a bowl of rice and a cup of drinking water and they all sat down around the fire to eat. Edna May sat down next to Kyle, who was sitting alone, and after he finished his prayer, Edna May said to him, "Thanks for sticking up for me last night."

"It was the right thing to do, Edna May," he said. "Justin had no right to disrespect you like that"

"Well, it was a real nice thing for you to do." she told him. I was kind of surprised that someone so...so... religious would be so...so..."

"Jesus loves you, Edna May," he told her. " Who am I to judge?"


When Vonda noticed Edna May heading for the porta potty, she waited a couple of minutes and then headed in the same direction. When Edna May came back out, Vonda was waiting for her.

"Thanks for last night," Edna May told her.

"No problem," she answered. "I wanted to slap the peckerhead, but I figured I'd get thrown out if I did. Anyway, I got your back, as long as you've got mine."

"Definitely," Edna May said. "Whatever you need."

"I think we may need each other," Vonda said. "You and I should form a secret alliance. We can help each other get to the final three. But, it's got to be a secret in order for it to work. We can't let anybody know that we're working as a team. You okay with that?"

"Yes, I am," answered Edna May. "I've seen enough reality shows to know that you have to have an alliance that you can trust, and I feel like I can trust you."

"Okay. Good," Vonda continued. "Here's what we'll do: after the first elimination we'll pull in two more campers.That way we'll have a majority. We'll let them think that we're four equal partners, though, so we don't have to worry about them turning on us. Deal?"

"Deal!" Edna May agreed.

"Okay, we'll talk more after the first elimination and figure out our plan then."


Vonda was itching to have a talk with Andrew, too, but Cassie was always hanging around him, so she used the same tactic she had with Edna May. She caught up with him as he was leaving the men's room and stopped him.

"I need to talk to you, Wordman. As far as this group goes, you're kind of like the…"

"The leader?" He asked.

"Yeah, the leader. Exactly. That's why I want to team up with you. We could form a secret alliance and work together to get to the final three. Nobody would ever suspect us of working together. I can help you run this game."

"You're right, Vonda. Nobody would ever suspect it. But we need numbers..."

"Yeah, I thought of that,' she told him. So...after the first elimination we work our way into a four-person alliance…

"And we'll be the majority. Brilliant!" he said.

"No one can know though," Vonda cautioned him.

"No," he agreed. "No one can know."

When Vonda returned from the bathroom Justin and Zeke were tossing a football around, Kyle was reading his Bible, Edna May was sweeping the tent and Nikki was sitting by the fire pit.

"Can you believe him?" Nikki asked as Vonda sat down next to her. "We get one small backpack each, and he takes up half of his with a football? And a frisbee?"

"Maybe that wasn't such a bad idea," Vonda told her. "At least it gives him something to do."

"Yeah, it gives him something to do alright," she said. "Something to do without me."

" I'm sure they'd let you play, if you wanted to," Vonda replied.

"I don't really want to throw a football around," Nikki answered. "That's not my idea of fun."

"Well, you could read Andrew's book," Vonda said.

Nikki rolled her eyes at the suggestion.

*Or you could sit around and feel sorry for yourself,* Vonda thought to herself.

"So where's the Professor and Maryanne at?" Vonda asked. Nikki pointed and said "They're over there exploring again."

Vonda could see them through the trees. Andrew appeared to be inspecting and commenting on every tree and plant he saw, and Cassie was right beside him and hanging on his every word. He pulled a couple of plants out of the ground and came running back to the camp with them in his hands.

"Look," he yelled."I found two wild onions."

"Put them in the cooking pot," Edna May told him as she exited the tent. "I'll use them in the rice tonight"

"Were so lucky to have someone at Camp Limbo with your knowledge, Andrew," added Cassie. "I just know we're going to need it."

Justin came running up to the firepit. He set the football on the ground and pulled off his shirt. He turned to Edna May and said, "Look what you're missing, Misty. Are you sure you don't want me to keep you warm tonight?"

"No, thank you," Edna May told him. "And my name is Edna May."

The sprinklers came on a short while later and the campers all hurried to get their buckets and collect water. After they were finished, Andrew doled out the day's ration of protein bars. He did a quick inventory and realized they were short one bar. *Maybe there's going to be a double eviction down the road*, he thought, so he didn't mention it to anyone.

After they ate their bars, Zeke and Jason went back to their football game. Kyle read his Bible while Vonda and Cassie read their copies of Andrew's book. Andrew sat on one of the rocks surrounding the fire pit and whittled a stick, while Edna May cleaned the pit and laid in fresh wood for later. Nikki sat alone across from Andrew and pouted.

"You're getting quite a sunburn," Andrew said to Edna May.

"I know," she answered. "I didn't think to bring any sunscreen."

"Cassie has sunscreen," Vonda mentioned.

"How do you know?" Cassie asked her. "Have you been poking around in my backpack?"

"No, I have *not* been poking around in your backpack," Vonda answered. "You came back from the bathroom this morning covered in grease. If it's not sunscreen, what is it?"

"It's not my fault that she forgot hers," Cassie said. "I have very fair skin and I can't risk running out. I don't think you can understand the problems that come with having white skin."

"I'm sure you're right," Vonda answered her. "Kinda like I can't understand the hardships you endure by being 'over-educated'."

"Exactly," Cassie said.

Vonda walked into the tent and came back out a minute later with a small plastic bottle. She handed it to Edna May and said, "Here's a sample of body lotion with sunscreen that I got from e-scentual's. You can have it."

"Oh, thanks, Vonda. That's so nice of you."

Edna May opened the bottle and started applying it to her shoulders.

"Wow," Edna May exclaimed, "this smells amazing."

"It's got jasmine, lavender and lime in it. The lime kind of balances the sweetness of the other two, don't you think?" Vonda asked.

"Yeah, and it feels great on my skin, too," Edna May told her. "If I win the $50,000, I'm going to order a ton of this," she added.

Cassie snorted.

Guillermo came through the huge wooden gate a short while later, pulling a child's red wagon behind him. Included in the wagon were two more sleeping bags, eight pieces of plywood measuring 1' x 1', and eight decks of playing cards. The campers could see that there was something else in the wagon, too, but it was covered by a sheet.

"Campers, it's time for your first individual reward challenge," he told them as he handed each camper a piece of plywood and a deck of cards.

"When I say go," he told them."you'll have four minutes to build a house of cards. Whoever has the highest building when the time is up, will win today's prize. Would you like to see what you're playing for?"

He pulled the sheet off the hidden item to reveal a KFC bag.

"There are six pieces of extra crispy chicken, a container of beans, a container of coleslaw and two biscuits in the bag. After the winner is determined, two more campers will have the chance to win sleeping bags by drawing cards. The two campers who draw the highest cards will win sleeping bags.

"Everybody ready?... One, two, three... go!"

All the campers got busy building their houses. Kyle had problems from the beginning, mainly because of his huge hands. He wasn't able to build it any higher than two stories. When Vonda put her fifth story on, her structure started to wobble, so she decided to stop.

"Vonda, are you holding at five stories?" Guillermo asked her.

"I am," she answered.

"We'll soon see if your strategy works," he said.

"Quitters never win," cried Justin, just as his seven-story house collapsed. Edna May was right behind him with six stories when hers collapsed  at the same time and she, too, had to start over. One by one, the other's houses collapsed, and at the end of four minutes Vonda had the tallest house.

Guillermo handed her the KFC bag and said, "You may pick one other camper to share your meal."

"Do I have to share?" she asked him.

"No, It's your choice," he answered.

She knew Edna May would be disappointed, but she said, "Thanks, I think I'll eat it by myself." She went and grabbed her copy of Andrew's book and then walked behind the trees, where she could eat her meal in peace.

"Vonda," Edna May called after her, "bring me back the bones."

"Why? You plan on sucking on the bones?" she asked.

"No, but I can boil them in the water and make a broth to cook the rice in," she told her.

"And could you bring the bag back, too?" Andrew asked. "I can use it when I forage."

After Vonda left to eat, Edna May, Nikki, Andrew and Cassie drew their Cards and Andrew and Cassie won the sleeping bags.

"Can we keep the cards?" Edna May asked.

"Sure," Will/Guillermo answered.


Vonda ate four pieces of the chicken, the container of coleslaw along and one of the biscuits. She wrapped the remaining biscuit and two pieces of chicken in napkins and stuck them in her pockets. She walked back to the camp and dumped the bones into the cooking pot. She took the container of beans out of the bag and handed them to Edna May.

"Here," she told her, "you can add these to the rice, too."

She gave the bag to Andrew. Much to his delight, she had left the extra plastic fork inside.


Vonda waited until Edna May had to use the restroom again, and then followed her. As she strolled toward the porta-potties, she heard Nikki say, "Boy, Vonda sure goes to the bathroom an awful lot." She realized then that she'd have to find a new way to have private conversations with her alliance members. When they were far enough away, Vonda slipped Edna May the chicken and biscuit.

"Eat fast and don't leave any traces," Vonda instructed her.

"Okay," Edna May answered. "And thank you! This was such a nice thing for you to do."

"I told you… we're a team. We just can't let anybody else know."

"Wow," Kyle said as he ate his second spoonful of rice, "this rice is a whole lot tastier than it was yesterday. Great job, Edna May. And thank you, Vonda, for sharing your beans."

"No problem," Vonda answered. "I don't really like beans," she lied.

"The beans help," Edna May admitted, "but the real thanks has to go to Andrew for the onions. It's the onions that add all the flavor."

Andrew beamed. Cassie snorted. Vonda smiled to herself and thought, *This girl is really playing the game, plus she's a lot smarter than the rest of them realize.*

Chapter 18

When the camera crew arrived at 6:00 the next morning they found Edna May already at work on getting the fire started. Kyle joined her shortly afterward, and the two of them sat and chatted while they waited for the rice to cook. Edna May thought that Kyle was a nice guy and she enjoyed his company. She felt bad for him, because he just didn't seem to fit in with the other campers. While the rest of the campers pretty much ignored him, Edna May made sure that she included him in her conversation. She could sense how lonely he was and she knew how that felt.

One by one, the other campers emerged from the tent, visited the porta-potty and sat down at the fire to eat. After breakfast the campers fell into what would be their usual routines. Andrew retrieved his KFC bag and went off to search for food with Cassie at his side. Edna May went to clean the tent. Vonda and Kyle were reading, and Nikki, Zeke and Justin sat under a tree playing cards.

"Has anyone approached either of you guys about forming an alliance?" Nikki asked Justin and Zeke.

"No," answered Justin. "How about you?"

"No," she told him."I wonder why."

"Because they're all morons," Justin told her. "They don't have any idea how to play this game. The three of us are together, though, right?"

"Yeah," Zeke said. "We're solid."

"We need a fourth member, though," Nikki told them. "So that we have a majority."

"How about Misty?" Justin asked.

"No," Nikki replied. Absolutely not!"

"What's the matter, Nikki?" asked Zeke. "Are you jealous of her?"

"No, I'm not jealous of *her*. But your poster girl is the biggest target here and she's not going to last long. Cassie hates her already and she'll probably do whatever it takes to get rid of her. And I think Andrew will go along with whatever Cassie wants to do."

"Vonda likes her," Justin told her. "She sure stuck up for her the other night."

"That's just because Vonda loves drama and she was looking for a fight. Vonda is only loyal to Vonda. After all, she didn't offer to share her chicken with Edna May did she?

"What you guys have to do is work on Kyle'" she continued. "Kyle's the perfect ally. He's got nobody else. You two have to make friends with him. He's clueless, so we can easily manipulate him."

"Hey, Kyle," Zeke yelled to him."You want to play some poker?"

"No, thanks," he answered. "I don't gamble."

"Dude, we're not really gambling. We're only using stones!" He told him.

"No, thank you."

Zeke looked at Nikki and shrugged."Well, I tried," he told her.

Nikki rolled her eyes at him and said, "Try harder."

Nikki walked over to where Kyle was sitting and asked him if there were any games that he enjoyed.

"Sure," he answered. "My family and I have 'Monopoly' marathons all the time."

Well,' she said, " in 'Monopoly' you play for fake money, right?"

"Yes."

"And we're playing for fake money, too. It's kind of the same thing, don't you think?" she asked.

"Maybe," he answered. "But I don't know how to play poker anyway."

"We'll teach you," she offered. "It'll be fun. And, besides, there's not much else to do here."

"Okay," he agreed. "I'll give it a try."

Nikki, Zeke and Justin gave Kyle a quick lesson and then began a game. Nikki had suggested to Justin and Zeke that they let Kyle win, at least a few hands, but they ignored her suggestion. It didn't really matter, because Kyle ended up winning all the stones.

"Beginners luck," Zeke grumbled as he walked away.


Guillermo showed up later that morning to host the competition.The campers were all anxious, because this competition would determine who went home first. The winner would get the day's prize and the two campers who performed the worst would be in danger of being voted out.

"Listen, Nikki told Justin and Zeke, "if you get a prize that you can share, make sure you choose Kyle."

Guillermo had the wagon with him again. In it he had two more sleeping bags with him and he gave them to Nikki and Edna May. He also had eight plastic spoons and 8 raw eggs with him and he handed one of each to the campers. For the challenge, they would have to march in a single file from the firepit to the tent while gripping the handle of the spoon between their teeth and balancing the egg on the other end. The first two campers to drop their eggs would be up for elimination, and the last camper with their egg intact would be

142

the winner. The prize was a six-cut pizza and two lukewarm Cokes. Guillermo explained that the winner could choose one, and only one, camper to share with.

Justin was behind Edna May, and he was so distracted by the view that he dropped his egg almost immediately. His egg splattered on the back of Edna May's leg, forcing her to flinch causing her to drop hers. The rest fell one by one until Zeke was the only one left with an egg.

"I'll be back tomorrow for our first campfire meeting," Guillermo announced, "where either Justin or Edna May will have their camping permit revoked and will be the first camper to leave Camp Limbo.

"Zeke, you won the competition. Would you like to pick another camper to share your meal with?"

"I gotta go with my bro, Justin," he answered.

Nikki shook her head and rolled her eyes at him. She realized then that it was up to her to save her alliance and get them to the final three. She'd have to pull Kyle in by herself. She'd have to start being friendlier to him. A lot friendlier.

While Zeke and Justin went off to eat their pizza behind some trees, the other campers settled down at the camp with their protein bars. Kyle sat down by the firepit and Nikki immediately joined him. She was determined to get him to join her alliance. Andrew went off to do some more exploring and

Edna May was organizing the supply locker. Vonda and Cassie went to sit under a tree together to read their copies of Andrew's book.

"Who are you thinking of voting out?" Vonda asked.

"Edna May, of course Cassie answered.

"Why 'of course'?" Vonda asked her.

"Because I'm not a hypocrite. I'm a feminist, and I can't condone what she does with her body. I have no respect for a woman like that."

"She's hardly a woman, Cassie. She's really just a kid. And we don't know what her circumstances were."

"It doesn't matter," Cassie said. "Most women wouldn't stoop that low under any circumstances. It's probably due to drugs or an abusive boyfriend. That's how these girls usually end up in that life."

Vonda called Edna May over to join them and said to Cassie, "Let's ask her."

Edna May walked over and sat down on the ground. Vonda asked her if she had ever had a drug problem.

"No," Edna May answered. "I've never done drugs."

Cassie snorted.

"Well," Edna May went on, "I did smoke weed a couple of times in high school to try and fit in. But that was it."

"Have you ever had an abusive boyfriend?" Vonda continued.

No," Edna May said. "I've dated a couple of guys, but I've never had a real boyfriend."

Cassie asked her, "So what made you decide to do porn?"

"It's kind of a long story," Edna May told her.

"Well, we've got lots of time," Cassie said.

"Look, if you'd rather not go into it….,"Vonda started.

"No, it's okay," Edna May said. "I'd kind of like to explain.

"See, my mother lost custody of me when I was 13 and I was put into foster care..."

"That's so sad," Vonda said.

"It wasn't that bad. In some ways it was better than being with my mother. She had some… um…*problems*. And I had some good and some not-so-good foster parents, but I was never abused or anything."

"So where was your father?" Cassie asked.

"I don't know," Edna May told her. "I never met him."

Cassie snorted again.

Vonda turned to Cassie and said, "Do you have a sinus condition?"

"No, I don't," she answered.

"Then stop with the annoying noises and let the girl finish her story."

"Anyway," Edna May continued, "it wasn't so bad the first couple of years. My mom and I had weekly visits and I got to spend time with her during holidays. She still had the same problems, though, so she decided to move out here to California and start fresh. I didn't see her for the next couple of years, but we Skyped and talked on the phone all the time. We planned that I would move out here after I aged-out of foster care. The day after I turned 18, my foster parents drove me to the airport and I flew out to live with my mom.

"It was nice to be reunited with her, but it wasn't perfect. She still had the same problems and was living with her boyfriend, Rick, who's a meth head. They only have a small one-bedroom apartment, so I was sleeping on the couch. I'd hoped to find a job and make enough for us to get a bigger place, but it was tough without a car. After a couple of weeks, I got a job in a coffee shop. The pay wasn't great, and it was only part-time, but the tips were decent and at least I was able to pay my fair share of the household expenses.

"I was working at the coffee shop for about a month when I waited on this guy, Peter. He told me that he produced videos and, for some reason, I thought he meant music videos. So when he asked me if I'd like to audition for him, I said yes. He gave me his card and we made an appointment to meet at 7 o'clock that evening at his studio. He said if I passed the audition, I could make up to $1000 a week!

"Anyway his videos turned out to be porn films about a group of girls getting drunk together and having sex. The girls would play sorority sisters, or cheerleaders, or nurses, for example. There was never any real plot. I didn't want to insult him, so I said I'd think about it and get back to him. And then I got out of there as fast as I could.

"I told my mother what happened and instead of agreeing that I did the right thing, she started yelling at me for turning him down! She said I should be willing to compromise for that kind of money!

"Rick came home later that night and when he got into bed with my mom she told him what had happened. He came tearing out of the bedroom, pulled me off the couch and started shaking me and screaming at me. He told me that they had welcomed me into their home, fed me and gave me a place to live and that I should be doing more to help out. I pointed out to him that I'm the one who cleans the place and that I buy and cook most of the food. That made him even angrier. He started hitting me and I fell down. Then it got really bad."

"Did he rape you,?" Cassie asked.

Edna May just stared into space for several seconds. Vonda was doing her best to channel the tough-as-nails Tonia Phillips and keep herself from crying.

"The worst part, though," Edna May went on, "is that my mother was in the next room and she never even tried to help me.

"Anyway after Rick went back to bed, I took a shower, got dressed, packed my backpack and left.

"I told my boss at the coffee shop a little of what happened and he found a nearby shelter that had room for me. I was only there a couple of hours when two girls jumped me and stole my backpack. I know it wasn't the right thing to do, but I didn't know where else to turn, so I called Peter. He arranged for me to share an apartment with two of his other actresses. It was really just one of those efficiency motels, and I was sleeping on the couch again, but I figured I'd only have to bear it for a few months until I could afford a car.

"It turned out that Peter had kind of exaggerated the amount of money I was going to get paid, so it took longer than I expected, but between my job with Peter and my job at the coffee shop I was able to buy a cheap car in about five months

"I got my car on the road on a Thursday and I went to the studio that same night to tell Peter that I was quitting. I wasn't scheduled to work that night... I never worked Thursday or

Friday nights, and I wasn't sure why,  because my roommates *always* worked those nights. But when I got there, I found out why. They weren't filming. There were all these men hanging out and… um… waiting for their turn with one of the *actresses*. It turned out that Peter was a pimp and some of the *actresses* were prostitutes!

"So I went back to the apartment, packed my backpack and left. I went back early the next day, when I knew Peter wouldn't be there yet. I wanted to warn the owner of the building, Joe, about what was going on after hours. Joe was a real nice man. I mean, he didn't even know that we were filming porn. Peter told him that we were making instructional videos for cheerleading teams. I hated lying to him, but I didn't want to ruin it for everybody else. But when I found out there was a illegal stuff going on, well, I really felt I had no choice.

"Joe thanked me for coming in and told me that he had been planning on talking to me about something He had a friend who owned a car dealership and the guy was looking for spokesmodel to do commercials and public appearances and stuff like that.  Joe had recommended me! Anyway, he told me that he was going to come back to his office later that night to see for himself what was going on. He called his friend and his friend agreed to come over, too, just to meet me. We planned to meet there at 8:00.

149

"I was so anxious that I got there way too early. I was parked in front of the studio, sitting in my car, and all of a sudden a bunch of police cars pull up. The next thing I know, they're bringing a group of people in handcuffs out of the building, and one of them was Joe! I tried to explain to some of the cops that Joe wasn't a part of it, but none of them would listen to me. I even called the police station, but I couldn't get anyone to talk to me."

"I'm confused," Cassie said. "Where were you planning on living?"

"In my car," Edna May answered. "My friend, Marshall, who was the baker at the coffee shop, said that I could stay at his place. I really appreciated the offer, but he and his boyfriend, Matt, live in a real tiny studio apartment. They'd have no privacy at all if I was there, so I wouldn't have felt comfortable. They did let me come over every day to take a shower and get something to eat, though.

"I spent all my free hours looking for a job. I filled out applications all over the place. I searched online, too. I had worked as a counselor-in-training at a YMCA camp for the last two summers, so I decided to look for a job as a camp counselor. It would have only been a seasonal job, but it would have given me a job and a home for the summer. I did a search and somehow I ended up on the Camp Limbo website. It was the last day that they were accepting applications, so I made a quick video, sent it in, and here I am!"


Joe was in his home office, watching the Camp Limbo feeds, when Corinne burst in through the door. She was in tears."

"You're the 'Joe', aren't you?" she asked him.

"I'm sorry, Corinne..."

"But..."

"I swear I had no idea she was a porn star," he told her.

"I know, Joe. But you have to help that poor child. She tried to help you."

"Help her how?" he asked her.

"I don't know, but you have to try. Talk to Will and the crew," she suggested.

"We *can't* interfere, Corinne. We can't damage the integrity of the show."

"It's a reality show Joe," Corrine answered. "There's no integrity in a reality show."


After Cassie went off in search of Andrew, Vonda told Edna May that they'd now have to put together their four-person alliance before the vote, and that Andrew and Cassie were their best bet to team up with.

"It might be too late, Vonda," Edna May told her. "And besides, Cassie hates me."

"Don't worry about Cassie," she told her. "Little Miss Feminist will probably vote whichever way Andrew does, and I'm pretty sure we can get Andrew on our side."

"What you have to do," Vonda went on, "is to make sure you have Kyle's vote. You were the only one who ever talked to him, and now Nikki, Zeke and Justin won't let him out of their sight. I know that they're just trying to get his vote, because they keep making fun of him behind his back."

"I've got an idea," Edna May told her, "but I'll need your help."

Edna May told Vonda her plan, and Vonda agreed that it just might work.

Nikki kept a close eye on Kyle for the rest of the day. She insisted that Zeke and Justin include him when they tossed the football around. When they were finished with their game, Nikki noticed Kyle walk behind a thick stand of trees. She waited until she was sure no one was watching her and then followed after him. When she caught up to him she asked, "What are you doing back here all by yourself? Did you want to be alone?"

"I came here to pray before making my decision on who to vote out," he informed her.

"I'm sure you'll do the right thing," she told him. "Justin is more of a friend to you than Edna May is. Besides, he's a better person. You have to decide which person you can trust and respect."

"But I hate being the one to crush someone's dream," he said.

"There can only be one winner, Kyle," she reminded him. " You can't save everybody. And, besides, most people have more than one dream. She'll get over it. Don't be sad."

"It's a big decision, Nikki, but that's not really why I'm sad," he replied. Kyle then told Nikki the story of his relationship with Christie.

"You might have dodged a bullet there," she told him when he finished. "You're better off living with her for a while first. Make sure that you're compatible before you get married."

"I couldn't live with a girl outside of marriage," he said. "It wouldn't be right. Did you and Zeke live together before you got married?"

"No, we didn't," she answered, "but I wish that we had. I might not have married him. My parents tried to convince me to move in with him for a while before I said 'yes' to marriage, but I didn't listen to them."

"Your parents encouraged you to live together?" Kyle said in surprise.

153

"Yeah," she answered. "It worked for them. What about your parents?"

"No! They would never do that. They're Christians. Christians don't believe in sex before marriage. Well, except for Christie."

"And are they happy?" she asked him.

"I suppose so," he answered. "I never really thought about it. They don't fight or yell at each other. The really seem to respect each other, too. They're certainly not *unhappy*."

"Well, my parents do occasionally fight with each other," Nikki said, "but I *know* they're happy together. Kyle, my father <u>never</u> leaves the house without kissing my mom goodbye. The only time Zeke kisses me is when he wants sex. And my dad brings my mom flowers almost every week. Zeke never brings me flowers….not even on Valentine's Day. My dad gets up and cooks breakfast for my mom every day. I can't even get Zeke to move somewhere where we'll have our own kitchen.

"I wanted a marriage like my parents have. Is that too much to ask for?"

"I don't think it's too much to ask for," Kyle answered. "And thank you. You've given me a lot to think about. And pray about."

When Joe walked into the control room, the crewmembers were all gathered around in a circle having some kind of a meeting.

"Am I interrupting something?" he asked.

"No, not at all," said Will. "Come on in."

"How's it going?" Joe asked.

"Well, I've got some good news and some bad news. I'll give you the good news first: the television writers just went on strike."

"How is that good news?" Joe asked.

"A lot of people who watch television shows like nighttime talk shows will be looking for something else to watch. There's a good chance that we could probably pick up a lot more viewers."

"And the bad news?"

"You probably already heard… Edna May's in danger of being evicted," Will answered. "and she's our most popular camper."

"Really? Edna May?"

"Yeah, haven't you read any of the message boards?" Will asked.

"I checked them out once. Those people are crazy."

"I know," Will agree. "But those crazy people are the ones who buy the feeds."

"Is there any way to save her?" Joe asked him.

"Were working on it, Mr. B.," Will answered, and then asked, "You're the 'Joe' that she was talking about, aren't you?"

"Yeah, I am," Joe told him. "Hell of a coincidence, isn't it?"

After everyone else had gotten into their sleeping bags that night, Edna May announced that she had to use the bathroom. Vonda waited until she had been gone for a few minutes and then called to Kyle, "Hey, Bible Boy....every time I start to fall asleep, I hear you snoring."

"I wasn't snoring. I'm not even asleep yet," Kyle protested.

"You were snoring. Now get out of the tent, and stay out until I fall asleep."

"But I wasn't snoring," he insisted.

"GET OUT OF THE TENT AND GET OUT OF MY FACE BEFORE I GET INTO YOURS!" Vonda yelled.

When Edna May returned from the bathroom, she found Kyle sitting on one of the rocks by the fire pit.

"What you doing out here by yourself, Kyle?" she asked him. "Can't you sleep?"

"Vonda kicked me out of the tent," he told her.

"She can't do that!" she told him.

"Well, she did it," he said.

"You have every right to be in the tent, Kyle. Just ignore her. Her bark is worse than her bite."

"Well, I don't like her barking at me, either," he complained.

Edna May sat on the rock next to Kyle.

"Well, I'm kinda glad I have a chance to talk to you alone," she told him. "I might be leaving tomorrow, and I wanted to thank you for being my friend. I feel so alone out here, and it helps to have someone who's so nice to me. Especially after the mistakes and bad decisions that I've made."

"I told you, Edna May, Jesus loves you and that's all that matters. Besides, I think you're a good person at heart."

"Thanks, Kyle. That means a lot to me. Could I ask you for a favor?"

"Sure," Kyle answered.

"Will you tell me more about Jesus?"

# Chapter 19

Vonda woke up early the next morning with intense stomach cramps. At first she thought it was her period, but she quickly realized the timing was all wrong. *Labor pains*, she thought to herself. *Ronda's in labor already. It's too soon...it's almost three weeks before her due date.* The pains only lasted a few minutes, though, so she figured it was a "false labor. *At least I hope that's all it is.* She was too worried to go back to sleep, so she decided to get the fire going. She wished she had paid more attention when Edna May built the fire, because she wasn't having much luck at first. It took her a few false starts before she eventually got a decent fire going. She put the water on to boil and went to the storage locker to get the rice. She remembered that Andrew had found some more wild onions, along with some dandelion greens, and she decided she'd add those, too. When she opened the locker, she was surprised to see an envelope sitting on top of the rice barrell. It read: **CAMP LIMBO SECRET ADVANTAGE.**

She tore the envelope open and read the enclosed note:

**THIS ADVANTAGE ENTITLES YOU TO SAVE ONE CAMPER WHO IS UP FOR ELIMINATION AND REPLACE HIM/HER WITH THE CAMPER OF YOUR CHOICE. THIS ADVANTAGE OFFER WILL EXPIRE WHEN THERE ARE ONLY FIVE CAMPERS LEFT.**

Vonda now had a chance to save Edna May, but she had to get Andrew to agree to the plan, and she had to do it fast. She grabbed a protein bar, stuck it in her pocket and started cooking breakfast. As soon as she saw Andrew emerge from the tent and head for the men's room, she followed after him. When she caught up with him, she showed him her advantage and said, "We have to save Edna May. Then we can pull her and Cassie into our alliance and send Justin home. We'll have the numbers then. But, nobody can know what we're up to, so I think I'm going to put you up as a pawn."

"Me?" Andrew asked. "Why me?"

"Because we definitely have the votes to save you, and we have to make sure that Justin goes home in order for our plan to work. We can't let those young guys steal the game. The only way we can guarantee that Cassie will vote out Justin, is if he's up against you. She'd never vote you off. And neither will Edna May, especially if I tell her that you offered to replace her."

"I don't know if I can do that," Andrew answered her.

"Do what?" Cassie asked as she came up behind them.

Vonda showed her the advantage and said, "I want to replace Edna May with Andrew, in order to assure that Justin goes home."

"Don't do it, Andrew," Cassie told him. "Don't put yourself in jeopardy."

"He's not in any jeopardy," Vonda said. "We have the votes to save him."

"You're asking too much," Cassie replied. She turned to Andrew and said, "You don't have to prove you're a nice guy, Andrew. Anyone can see that just by the way you take care of us and by the love and respect that you show your grandmother."

"My grandmother?..." he asked.

"Yes, your Nan."

"Nan's not my grandmother," he told her. "Nan's my wife!"

"Your wife??" Cassie asked, surprised. "You're married?"

*Uh-oh*, thought Vonda. *Time to quickly change the subject and do some damage control.*

"Andrew,' Vonda asked him, "what would Alex do?"

Andrew thought about it for a few seconds and answered, "I'll do it! I'll fall on my sword to save the fair maiden." And then strode off.

Cassie watched him walk away and then turned back to Vonda. "If you put him up now, I'll vote him off," she told her.

"You don't want to do that, Cassie," she cautioned her.

"Are you threatening me?" Cassie asked.

"No, of course not. If I was threatening you, you wouldn't have to ask. I'm trying to help you."

"But he lied to me, Vonda, He led me on. He never even mentioned that he was married."

"Yes, he did," Vonda lied. "But you can't blame him for not talking about his wife in front of you. He's obviously crazy about you."

"You really think so?" Cassie asked.

"I know so," Vonda went on. "Just the way he looks at you. And *listens* to you. Everybody sees it. And just imagine how the viewers see it: Two people, who seem to be made for each other, yet it's……"

"A forbidden love!" Cassie exclaimed. "How romantic!"

"Exactly," Vonda said.

"We're like Romeo and Juliet."

"Well, not quite." Cassie said, "That didn't turn out so well. You're more like a modern-day Jane Eyre."

"Yes, you're right," Cassie agreed. "And his wife is *old*, so…."

"I don't know if I'd go there, Cassie," Vonda warned her. But I'll bet there's a lot of single men who are watching and hoping to save you from this doomed romance."

"You might be right," Cassie said. "I'm the victim here."

"Sure," Vonda told her. "And you can use Andrew's feelings for you to advance in the game. I'm thinking that you and I should form a secret alliance. Nobody would *ever* suspect it. We can team up with Andrew and Edna May, and we'll have the majority. We can help each other get to the final three."

"But why would I want to team up with Edna May?" Cassie asked her.

"Because,' Vonda explained, "if we save her, she'll owe us. We'll control her and her vote."

"And what about Kyle?" Cassie asked.

"That's the beauty of our plan," Vonda said. "Kyle will vote with Edna May, so we'll control him and his vote, too. But if Edna May leaves, Kyle might flip to the other side and then they'll have the numbers.

"Cassie, you and I, two strong *feminists*, can run this game until we're in the final three, and none of these other campers will know what hit them."

"Wow. You're right, Vonda. "How did you get to be so smart?"

"I guess I don't have the *disadvantage* of being over-educated," Vonda replied.

"You're probably right. I suppose that you grew up in a way that I can't even imagine. You must have had to develop your street smarts at a young age"

*Yeah*, thought Vonda. *Growing up on the mean streets of Garden Grove really forced me to hone my survival skills.*

When Vonda returned to camp, Edna May was sweeping the tent, while the other campers sat around the fire pit. Vonda entered the tent and stashed the protein bar while Edna May's back was turned. She walked back out and gestured to Kyle to follow her into the tent. When he didn't respond, she glared at him until he did. When they were inside the tent, she said to him, "Look, Kyle, I'm sorry for the way I treated you last night. I know it's no excuse, but I'm hungry and tired and on edge. I'm really sorry that I took it out on you."

"I understand," he responded. "And I appreciate and accept your apology."

"Thanks, Kyle. Listen, why don't you and I move the sleeping bags out of the way for Edna May, so she can finish sweeping. I'll do the right side, and you can do the left side."

Kyle started to collect the sleeping bags. When he picked up Justin's, he found two protein bars hidden underneath. Vonda's insurance had paid off.

"Justin's been stealing food," he cried and held the two bars out for Edna May and Vonda to see.

"Wow," said Vonda. "I can't believe anyone would be that low. I don't think we should confront him, though. We don't need the drama and we sure don't need a fight. Let's just vote him out!"

After Vonda finished helping Edna May clean the tent, she took her copy of Andrew's book and joined Cassie where she was sitting under a tree and reading. Andrew strolled over and sat down.

"How do you like it so far?" he asked them.

"I'm almost done," Vonda told him."In fact, I'm on page eight hundred and thirty two, and I still don't get the plot."

"Plot?" he said. "There's no *plot*. It's not a murder mystery. It's a *story*. With a message...a moral story."

"And what would that moral be?" Vonda asked him.

"That your success in life is determined by the choices you make," he answered.

"Well, I'm enjoying it," Cassie offered. I think your character, Alex, is a man to be admired. A role model, in fact. Is it autobiographical by any chance?" she asked.

"Ah…semi-autobiographical, perhaps," he answered her.

"I thought so," Cassie told him. "I thought I detected a bit of Andrew in Alex."

"Well it sure is wordy, Wordman," Vonda said.


The campers were all sitting around the fire pit, eating their protein bars when Will came strolling through the gate pulling the wagon. He brought the wagon up to the fire pit and greeted the campers.

"First things first," he said. "This is our first campfire meeting and someone will lose their camping permit today. That camper will be driven to Los Angeles where they'll be taken to the Bradley Inn for a one night stay in one of their luxurious rooms. You'll also be given $100 in cash to spend any way you choose. You'll have the opportunity to dine in one of the Bradley Inns' three great dining establishments. Or you can order poolside service at the Bradley Inn's beautiful, covered patio.

"Now will the two campers at risk please come stand next to me?"

Edna May and Justin got up from the rocks they were sitting on and went to stand on either side of Will. Vonda also rose from her rock. She walked over to Will and handed him her advantage. Will read it aloud to the campers and then asked Vonda if she wanted to use it.

"Yes, I do," she told him."I want to save Edna May and put Andrew up."

"Okay." Will said. "Edna May, you can sit back down. Andrew I need you to come up here with Justin and me."

Edna May, Justin, Nikki, Zeke and Kyle were all shocked by the unexpected turn of events. Cassie pretended that she was shocked and Andrew, being Andrew, overacted his surprise at being nominated. Luckily, thought Vonda, no one seemed to notice.

Will/Guillermo walked around the fire pit and asked each camper for their vote. Zeke and Nikki were the only campers to vote against Andrew, so Justin was the first camper voted out. Vonda's plan had worked.

"Justin you have 10 minutes to pack your belongings and say your 'goodbyes'. Your driver will meet you at the gate, where you'll be blindfolded and driven back to LA. Adios, Justin."

Nikki won that day's competition, which consisted of balancing the 12" x 12" piece of plywood from the house of cards challenge on her head. Her prize was two peanut butter and jelly sandwiches and two cans of warm beer. She chose to share with Kyle, which angered her husband.

"I told you we have to have Kyle on our side," she explained to him when he complained. "We need him more than ever now that Justin's gone."

Zeke refused to talk to her for the rest of the day, which didn't bother her a bit. It gave her the opportunity to hang out with the other campers, particularly Kyle, and try to develop relationships with them. She couldn't count on Zeke to save them. She'd have to try to save herself.

Nikki and Kyle strolled off into the trees to eat their sandwiches. "I don't drink alcohol," Kyle said when Nikki handed him one of the beers.

"That's pretty rude," Nikki said. "You should have spoken up sooner, Kyle, so I could have picked someone who would have appreciated it."

"I'm sorry, Nikki," he told her, "but I don't believe in using drugs or alcohol."

"Then just drink half of it. It would be a sin to waste the calories."

Kyle did as directed and took a sip of beer. He made a face and said, "I don't like the taste."

"That's just because it's warm," she told him. "Keep drinking...it'll taste better after the first few sips."

Joe met up with Will when Will was walking from the campsite to the control center.

"Hey, that was great!," Joe said. "I still can't believe Vonda used her save on Edna May."

"I know," Will answer. "We put it in the rice barrel, because Edna May's the only one who ever cooks. Vonda threw a wrench into our plans, but it worked out even better than we expected."

"Corinne's going to be happy," Joe told him. "By the way," he asked, "what's the deal with The Bradley Inn?"

"My friend's father owns it," Will told him, "and I made a deal with him. He agreed to give us the free room if we gave them free publicity. It's a win-win."

"That *is* a good deal," Joe agreed.

"Cam's going to stop and pick up some pizzas and beer after he drops Justin off," Will added. "Why don't you come over to the studio in a couple of hours and celebrate with us?"

"A couple of hours? Does he really have to travel the whole route back?"

"Yeah. Justin can't know where he was. If anyone finds out, we'll have fans hanging out all over the place. Nobody can know they're here, Mr. B. That's real important."

"I sure won't say anything", Joe told him. "And I know Corinne won't, but I worry about my kids telling their friends."

"Oh, they won't say anything, either. I made sure of that," Will told him.

"How?"

"I told them that if anyone finds out, you could go to jail."

"What! I thought you said this was legal?" Joe asked.

"I said I didn't think it was *illegal*. But I'm not a law student, Mr. B."

"I can't afford to get in anymore legal trouble, Will. I can't take that chance."

"Don't worry, Mr. B. If anything happens, and it won't, just say you rented the studio apartment to me, and that you had no idea what was going on."

"Sure," Joe said. "That makes me feel better. Because the last two times I used that defense, it worked out so well for me."

Chapter 20

Someone downloaded a video clip on YouTube of Edna May telling her life story and it quickly went viral. Joe wasn't sure if the video, the TV writers strike, or a combination of the two were responsible, but subscriptions doubled before the first week was over, and they kept coming in. Joe couldn't believe how profitable Camp Limbo was. Maybe Corinne would be more comfortable having the kitchen redone after he showed her the final numbers.

Interest in the show grew daily. When Justin had shown up at The Bradley Inn after his eviction, there had been a few reporters from some online gossip/celebrity sites waiting for him. The number of reporters grew with each eviction. After the third eviction, the crew had to make arrangements with the staff of The Bradley Inn to sneak the campers in, using different service doors and garage entrances each time. They didn't mind if the campers spoke to reporters, but they wanted to make sure that the drivers remained anonymous and that no one followed them back to Camp Limbo.

During the second week of the show, *People* magazine published a short article titled 'Where is Camp Limbo?', which included an interview with Justin. He was quoted as saying "We were told that we were being driven two hours north of Los Angeles, but I think that bit of information was a red herring. It seems like we were in those cars much longer than that. I've got a good sense of direction, though, so I'm pretty sure that we did travel north the whole way."

Joe was sitting at his desk, reading the *People* magazine article when he got a phone call from his friend, Sam. Joe and Sam had been best friends since the days when they played on the same Little League team together. Sam had gone to work at his father's car dealership after high school, and after several years of working for his father he decided to strike out on his own. He moved to Los Angeles and opened a used-car lot. He

171

dealt only in luxury cars and after a couple years of hard work and smart deals, he had built up a successful business. Corinne, Joe and the kids had visited him one year for their vacation, and they enjoyed themselves so much, that they decided to move there themselves.

"Joe," he greeted him."How are you doing? I've been meaning to call you since Kara's graduation party to tell you what a good time we had. It's a shame we don't get together more often."

"Thanks Sam," Joe replied. "I'm sorry that we couldn't come to your Fourth of July party this year, but you know I can't go anywhere."

"Yeah, I'm sorry, too. We missed having you guys here.

"I was wondering, Joe," Sam continued, "have you heard about that web show, Camp Limbo?"

"Yeah, I have," Joe answered cautiously. "I've seen some clips of it. Why?"

"That girl, Edna May, she's the one you wanted to audition for me, isn't she?"

"Yeah, that's her," Joe told him. "And I'm sorry about that. I swear I had no idea that she was a porn star."

"That doesn't matter. Do you still know how to get in touch with her?" Sam asked him.

"Isn't she still at that camp?" Joe asked.

"Yeah. I mean when she gets out. Can you get in touch with her?" Sam asked again.

"I think so," Joe replied. "Why?"

"Because I want to hire her," Sam answered."

"But she's an ex-porn star!" Joe said.

"I know," Sam told him. "And she's also 'America's Sweetheart' right now. I want to sign her before someone else does. You know, before her 15 minutes are up."

"I think I can get ahold of her," Joe told him.

"Thanks, Joe. If you can do this for me, I'll owe you one."

Although the campers collected fresh water daily, after they set enough aside for drinking and cooking, there was rarely any left over for bathing. Edna May's wet wipes weren't really an effective alternative, so Vonda took the opportunity to introduce the campers and the viewers to e-scentuals body sprays.

"We may not be clean," she told them, "but we can at least smell good."

She passed around sprays in several different fragrance combinations, and she let the campers choose their favorites. She made sure several times a day to remark on how nice everyone smelled.

There wasn't much to do at Camp Limbo, so the campers looked forward to the competitions each day. The challenges weren't very complicated - one consisted of shooting paper cups with a water pistol, and another was popping balloons with darts - but the rewards of food were desirable enough to inspire the campers to play hard. The rewards were always food of some sort, ranging from coffee and doughnuts to strip steaks and potatoes. There was usually enough to share with at least one other camper, and everyone but Vonda shared their win. However, Vonda continued to sneak food to Edna May whenever she could.

For the contest on day seven, the campers had a scavenger hunt and the prize was a can of chicken noodle soup. Andrew won the soup and, much to Cassie's chagrin, he chose to share it with Edna May, because she was the only camper who had not won any food to date. Nikki and Zeke came in last that day, which meant that one of them would be going home next.

Vonda waited until she could speak to Cassie in private and then asked her, "What you think we should do about the vote? I'll go along with whatever you decide."

"I think we should vote Zeke off," Cassie answered.

"Okay, then that's the plan. Is there a reason you'd rather vote Zeke over Nikki?" she asked her.

"I just don't like him," Cassie told her.

"Do you think he's the smarter of the two?" Vonda asked.

"No. No way. I don't think he's smart at all," Cassie replied. "In fact, I think he's pretty dumb."

"So you think we should keep the smarter one? You aren't afraid that she'll figure out that you and I are running things?"

"I never thought of that," Cassie told her.

"I'm probably worrying about nothing," Vonda told her "If you want Zeke to go, I'll vote for Zeke. It's your call."

"Well, maybe we should vote Nikki out, just in case," Cassie decided. I have noticed how she watches everyone. And I've noticed the way she sucks up to Kyle all the time."

"Are you sure?" Vonda asked her. "Because I want to make sure that you and I are on the same page."

"Yes, I'm sure," Cassie declared. "Let's vote out Nikki. I'll get Andrew on board and you work on Edna May," Cassie told her.

"Okay," Vonda said."I think you're probably right."


Vonda had Phase One of her plan in place and for the next part she needed to talk to Zeke. She approached him right after her conversation with Cassie.

"How badly do you want to stay?" she asked him.

"I really, really want to stay," he told her. "What do you think my chances are?"

"I think I can help you," she told him, "but you can't tell anyone, or the whole thing will blow up in our faces. If I can arrange for the campfire meeting to go your way, you have to promise me that you'll vote however I tell you to at the next one."

"No problem," he said. "I'm okay with that."

After they had finished their breakfast of rice the next morning, Nikki asked Zeke to take a private walk with her behind the trees. When they were alone, she put her arms around him and said, "I'm going to miss you."

"I'm going to miss you, too, babe," he told her. "But I'll be home in less than two weeks, hopefully $50,000 richer."

"What do you mean 'you'll be home'?" she asked him. "You might be the one leaving today."

"No, it's going to be you, Nikki," he told her.

"How do you know?" she asked him.

"I just know," he answered.

"Zeke, tell me! *How* do you know?"

"I made a deal," he told her.

"With who?" she asked him.

"I can't tell you. That's part of the deal."

"I can't believe you threw me under the bus and made a secret deal without me. I'm your wife, for crying out loud. We're supposed to be in this together."

"It's a game, babe. I don't show you my hand when we're playing cards, do I? It's the same thing. Besides, only one of us can win and I've got a better chance than you. I'm way more athletic, so I can probably do better in the challenges."

"Seriously, Zeke? You think you have superior squirt gun skills?" she asked him sarcastically.

"I also have better people skills," he told her. "I mean, which one of us has more friends?"

"I think I do," she answered.

"Oh, c'mon, Nikki. I always have friends over. I hardly ever see your friends around," he said.

"That's because my friends have better things to do than hang out in your mother's basement," she told him.

"Babe, I'm the one who was able to save myself," he pointed out. "I've got a deal going, Nikki, unlike you. I could win this thing. And what difference does it make which one of us wins?"

"Maybe you're right," she answered. "As long as one of us comes home with the money we can get our tiny house."

"Or a motorcycle," he said.

"A motorcycle? But our dream is a tiny house."

"No, Nikki," he replied. "That's your dream."

Chapter 21


Vonda's plan had worked. Nikki was the next camper to be voted out. The vote was unanimous. Zeke won the competition that day by bouncing the most rubber balls into a bucket, and he chose to share his loaded nachos with Vonda, a move that surprised everyone in camp except for Vonda.

The campers at Camp Limbo were hungry, tired and dirty, but mostly they were just bored. Andrew managed to keep busy by searching the campsite for wild onions, dandelion greens and anything else he thought could be used to flavor the rice, and Edna May kept to her usual routine of cooking and cleaning the tent. The others spent most of their time sitting around the fire pit or napping. Even so, viewer subscriptions kept increasing. Joe had to admit that watching the campers could get pretty boring at times, but just like the internet audience, he was hooked.

On the morning of day eleven, the campers were sitting around the fire pit eating their morning rice and speculating on who would lose the competition that day and risk eviction, when Edna May said, "It might not matter who loses, anyway. I'm thinking about leaving."

"Why?" asked Andrew.

"Because I'm hungry and I'm tired," she answered. "And I'd love to be able to spend one night in a clean bed and eat a real meal. And be able to take a shower. And sleep with a pillow. But mostly because I'm hungry."

Andrew held out his bowl to her and said, "Here, I'll share my rice with you if it will help you change your mind. I really think you should stay."

Vonda said, "C'mon, Edna May. You can do this."

Zeke said, "Let her go. It's one less person to beat."

Cassie snorted.

Kyle said, "If Edna May goes, I go, too."

Edna May glared at him. "Don't you dare," she told him. "If you quit because of me, I'll never speak to you again!"

Edna May stormed off and Vonda waited a few minutes before following her. She knew where she'd find her. Andrew had used his high-power binoculars to locate all the cameras that were hidden in the trees, and he soon realized that the only camera-free zones, aside from inside the bathrooms, were the areas behind the bathrooms. Neither the viewers nor the other campers could see back there, although the viewers could hear the conversation. It was the closest thing to privacy that could be found at Camp Limbo, and the campers took advantage of it. This time, though, one of the camera operators followed Vonda, assuming that there was going to be a scene that the viewers would want to see.

Vonda walked behind the bathrooms and was surprised that Edna May wasn't there.

"I'm up here," Edna May called down to her. She was sitting on a tree branch, directly above Vonda's head.

"You're not really going to quit, are you?" Vonda asked her.

"I don't know. Sometimes I feel like I'm just running away from my problems and postponing the inevitable. When I leave here, I still won't have a  job. I still won't have a place to live. I really don't believe that I have much of a chance to win the money, either. What if I'm missing all kinds of opportunities while I'm here?"

"But what if this *is* your opportunity?" Vonda asked her.

"Listen," Vonda went on, "there's something I've been wanting to talk to you about. I have a spare bedroom at my place, and I really want you to come and live with me when we get out of here. It's already furnished, and you'd have your own bathroom."

"Oh, Vonda, I couldn't ask you to do that," Edna May insisted.

"You're not asking me, sweetheart. I'm inviting you."

"Why?"

"Because you're my friend, and that's what friends do," she answered. "I never told you this, but I'm a twin. My sister, Ronda, and I have always lived together until about a year ago. We shared a bedroom together when we were kids, even though we didn't have to. We went to the same college and rented our first apartment together after graduation. Ronda got married last year, and she's due to have her first baby any day now. We're still as close as we ever were, but our lives are going in different directions now. I've never lived alone before, and I hate it. I think you and I would be good roommates. I can probably even help you find a job. I know a lot of business owners.

"Think about it, okay?" she added.

"Vonda," Edna May asked, "if I do move in, can we get a kitten?"

*Boy,* thought Vonda, *she really is just a kid.*

"Sure, sweetheart, we can get a kitten."

Joe rushed over to the studio and found the crew in panic mode after hearing Edna May announce that she was considering quitting the show.

"Double the prize money," Joe told Will.

"Are you sure, Mr.B... $100,000? That's a lot of money."

"Are you kidding?" Joe answered. "Have you seen the subscriptions? We're making money hand over fist," Joe answered.

"Okay, Mr. B., whatever you say. It's your money."

The increased prize money, along with the possibility of a real home, were enough to convince Edna May to stick it out. Zeke and Cassie lost the competition that day, which consisted of shooting Nerf guns at plywood targets. Andrew came in first and won a jumbo bucket of popcorn, which he happily shared with the other campers. He was distressed by how hungry everyone was, especially Edna May. He wanted to be the camp leader and provider. He felt like he was failing in that role. He didn't know what more he could do, though. *What would Alex do?* he thought to himself, and then a plan began to take shape.

182

The next day, after distributing the protein bars, Andrew dumped the remaining bars out of the crate and into the bottom of the storage chest. He searched the campsite until he found a stick in the right size and then he cut a long piece of a vine. He fashioned a rudimentary trap from the three items by propping the crate up with the stick and tying one end of the vine to the stick. He positioned it behind a strand of trees. He had saved a handful of popcorn from his reward, and he placed them inside the trap. Then he took the other end of the vine, sat back against a tree and waited. In less than 10 minutes, he had caught a squirrel in his trap. He took out his knife, approached the crate.... and chickened out. He hurried back to the fire pit where all the campers, with the exception of Edna May were still gathered.

"I trapped a squirrel!" he exclaimed.

"Why?" asked Cassie.

"Ah... for dinner," he answered.

"I ain't eating no rodent meat, Wordman," Vonda told him.

"Squirrel meat is tasty," Kyle told her. "Lots of people eat squirrel."

"No, lots of people do *not* eat squirrel," she replied. "I have never eaten squirrel and nobody I know has ever eaten squirrel. A squirrel is just a rat with a bushy tail. It's a like tree rat!"

"It could be a ground squirrel," Kyle said.

"It's still a rodent, no matter where it lives," Vonda replied. "And I don't eat rodents."

"Come on, Vonda," Zeke said. "your people eat chitlins."

"My people? MY PEOPLE!? You think we *all* eat chitlins? Boy, you really are a peckerhead, Zeke," she told him.

"I can dress a squirrel," Kyle offered."Where is it?"

"It's behind that copse," Andrew told him and pointed in the general direction.

"What the hell is a copse?" Vonda asked.

"That group of small trees," he told her and pointed again.

"Then why not just say 'that group of trees'?" Vonda asked him.

"Geez," Kyle said, "even I know what a 'copse' is."

"Yeah," said Vonda, "but you're still a rodent eater."


The campers followed Andrew to the spot where he had trapped the squirrel. When they got there, they found Edna May sitting on the ground next to the crate, pulling peanuts off her protein bar and feeding them to the squirrel through the slats.

"How did the squirrel get in the crate?" she asked.

"I trapped it," Andrew answered proudly.

"Wow! That's amazing," she told him.

Andrew beamed, until Edna May said, "But we're going to let it go, right?"

184

"No." Kyle answered."We're going to have it for dinner."

He took Andrew's knife and came toward the crate. Edna May draped herself over the top of the crate and said, "No! Stop right there, Kyle. You can't kill Felicia."

"Felicia? You named the squirrel?" Kyle asked her.

"Yeah, I did. I thought she was going to be like our pet or something."

Andrew's heart sank. He was trying to be the hero here, but his plan was falling apart. Before anyone could stop her, Edna May lifted the crate and released the squirrel, which scooted up the nearest tree.

"Definitely a tree squirrel," Kyle added.

Edna May brought her protein bar to the same spot the next day. She picked off the peanuts and left them in a pile on the ground. She sat back against a nearby tree and waited until the squirrel appeared and began eating the nuts. Now, one tree squirrel looks just like any other tree squirrel, but Edna May was convinced that it was Felicia. She came back every day after that, and she soon had the squirrel eating out of her hand.

Zeke was the next camper voted out, and Kyle followed four days later. Edna May cried when she had to cast her vote, even though she had warned him ahead of time. "I'm so sorry," she had told him, "but I've been in a final four alliance with them since the first couple of days. I gave them my word."

"I understand," he told her. "And thanks for the heads-up. Thanks for being my friend, too. I've learned a lot from you and all the other campers here. Before I came to Camp Limbo, I never in a million years would have tried drinking beer or gambling. And I sure wouldn't have ever hung out with a porn star."

"Ex-porn star," she corrected him.

"It doesn't matter," he told her, "Porn star, ex-porn star....it just doesn't matter. You're one of the sweetest people I've ever met, Edna May, and you've taught me to be a lot more open-minded about the people that I let into my life. I'll really miss you."

"I'll miss you, too, Kyle," she told him. "I'll see you on Facebook."


Vonda's strategy had worked and her alliance had made it to the final four. There was only one more elimination competition before the viewers took control and began voting for the winner.

Chapter 22

Edna May was dreaming about bacon. She dreamt that she
was in a strange house, searching room by room for the
kitchen, because she was hungry and she could smell bacon
frying. She slowly came awake and realized she really *could*
smell bacon. Somebody was cooking bacon nearby. She got
out of her sleeping bag, quietly grabbed Andrew's flashlight and
binoculars and left the tent. The camp was quiet and empty.
There were still a couple of hours before the camera crew was
due.

She made her way to the spot behind the bathrooms and climbed the tree. She couldn't see anything from her usual perch, but the aroma was getting stronger. She climbed as high as she dared and she found a strong branch from a tree on the other side of the wall that would safely hold her weight. From there she could see a steep hill leading down to a large outdoor area with well-manicured grounds. There was a huge in-ground pool with a surrounding patio, and to the left of the pool was a tree-lined walkway that led up a small hill. She couldn't see where the path ended, but she thought it might be a luxury hotel or resort. To the right of the pool was an area surrounded by high-power lights, with a large metal container in the center. She trained Andrew's binoculars on that area and realized almost immediately what she was seeing.

Edna May ran back to the tent and gently shook Andrew until he was awake. She motioned for him to keep quiet and to follow her. He started to grab his mic, and she shook her head. "Bring your knife and your bag," she whispered to him. When they were outside of the tent she explained to him that there was a whole pig being roasted on the other side of the wall. She was planning on sneaking onto the grounds to cut off some of the meat, and she wanted Andrew to act as a lookout. Andrew persuaded her that he should be the one to go. He was convinced that he could cut and carry more meat than she could. *Plus*, he told himself, *it was what Alex would do.*

Edna May led Andrew up the tree and then sat on a branch and waited while Andrew ran down the hill and into the yard. She watched him through the binoculars as he feverishly sliced strips of meat off the pig. It seemed like he was taking forever, but in reality he was gone less than ten minutes.

After Andrew returned over the wall with the bag of pork, he and Edna May hurried back to camp to hide the meat before the camera crew arrived for the day. They realized that the night vision cameras had picked up some of their movements, but they hoped that any viewers that may be watching would be more confused than suspicious They stored the meat in the storage locker and then retrieved their mics. They got the fire going and sat and talked while they waited. The camera crew arrived at 6:00 a.m., and Vonda and Cassie emerged from the tent shortly afterwards. Edna May waited until they were all seated around the fire pit before she went to get the rice from the storage chest. She opened the chest and cried "Oh my god. We've got meat!"

"Meat?" asked Vonda."Let me see."

Vonda ripped a piece of skin off of the half-cooked meat and popped it in her mouth."It's pork," she told them. "I don't know who might have put it here, but thank you, thank you, thank you! And I don't want to sound ungrateful, but what we need now is some barbecue sauce. If you're listening, Guillermo, or whoever, could you bring us some barbecue sauce. Wouldn't it be sweet to simmer that pork in some barbecue sauce? C'mon, do us a favor."

Edna May had been looking for a chance to do something special for Vonda, so after she added the rice and meat to the boiling water she headed for the spot behind the bathrooms. She left her mic at the foot of the tree and climbed up and over until she was outside the wall. She didn't want to take the same route that Andrew had taken. It had still been dark out when he ran down the hill, but the sun was shining brightly now, and there was nowhere to hide on that side. She took a chance and walked in the other direction around the wall. When she came around to the other side, she saw another, smaller pool and patio area. There was a small pool house to the right of the pool, and she could see the outside of the gate to Camp Limbo behind it. There was a large house to the left. She was in somebody's backyard.

She sneaked up to the house and peeked in a sliding glass door from the patio. She was looking into a living room or a family room, and she could see that there was a doorway to a kitchen on the left. She watched through the windows for a couple of minutes and didn't see any movement inside, so she took a chance and tried the door. It was unlocked. She entered the house as quietly as possible and tiptoed across the family room toward the kitchen. When she walked through the kitchen doorway, she came face-to-face with Joe.

"Misty?"

"Joe? What are you doing here?" she asked him. "And it's Edna May."

"I live here," he answered. "What are you doing here?"

"Looking for barbecue sauce," she answered.

"How did you get out?" he asked.

"I climbed a tree," she told him."

"Did anybody see you?"

"No."

"You gotta go back, Edna May, before you ruin everything. And you can't tell anyone you were here. Geez, this could screw up the whole thing."

"I'm sorry, Joe. I was just trying to do something nice for Vonda, but I don't want to mess things up or get you in trouble or anything."

"Good. Thanks. But before you go, I've got some good news for you. Remember my friend, the guy I told you about that has a car dealership? He's been watching the show and he wants to hire you as a spokesmodel when you get out."

"Really?"

"Yeah, but you gotta get back before you screw the whole thing up," he warned her.

"Okay. Thanks, Joe."

Just then Joe heard raised voices coming down the hall. He motioned for Edna May to hide in the pantry just as Corinne and Martin entered the kitchen.

"Joe, will you tell this idiot that we didn't take his pig," Corinne said.

"I didn't even know you had a pet pig," Joe told Martin. "And why would we take your pig?"

"It wasn't a pet pig...it was a *roasting pig*. Someone snuck into the pool area and sliced hunks off of it while the caterers were setting up the tables and chairs on the terrace," Martin explained.

*Uh-oh*, Joe said to himself.

"I'll tell you what," Joe said, "if I see anyone running around the neighborhood carrying pieces of pork, I'll let you know. But in the meantime, get off my property before I call the police."

"We don't need to involve the police," Martin told him. "I'm leaving. I'll see myself out."

"No, I'll see you out," Corinne said.

"What's Earl Martin doing here?" Edna May asked Joe when she came out of the pantry?"

"That guy's an earl? And how do you know an earl?" Joe asked.

"He's not an earl. He's just Earl. Earl Martin. He's married to my aunt Lettie."

"Letitia is your aunt?" Joe asked her.

"Her real name is Lettie. Letitia is one of the names she uses when she's running one of her scams."

"That's why she looked so familiar to me," Joe told her. "She looks like an older version of you."

Edna May quickly filled Joe in on Lettie and Earl's history.

"Are you sure about all this?" he asked her when she had finished her story.

"Yes, I'm sure. I'm positive. They've got at least two warrants out for their arrests that I know of. Joe, I've got to go to the police and warn them. Somebody could be in real danger."

"Don't worry...I'll make sure the police are called," Joe told her. "You get back to camp as fast as you can."

Edna May turned and headed for the door just as Corinne came back into the kitchen.

"What's she doing here?" Corinne asked.

"Looking for barbecue sauce," Joe told her.

"No! This can't be happening." Corinne replied.

Corinne went to the refrigerator, pulled out a bottle of barbecue sauce and handed it to Edna May. "I don't want to know why you want the barbecue sauce, and I don't want to know how you got out, but you better get back in as quickly as you can and you better make sure that nobody sees you."

"Okay,' Edna May answered, " and thank you for the…"

"***GO!***"


After Edna May left, Joe grabbed his phone, sat down at the kitchen table  and dialed his attorney's emergency number. While he was waiting for him to answer, he turned to Corinne. "Sit down," he told her. "I think you should listen to this call."

"Hello," said a voice on the other end. "This is Sid. I'm about to tee off, so this better be important."

"It is," Joe replied. "In fact, it could be a matter of life and death. I need to call in an anonymous tip to the police."

"I've got caller ID, Joe. I know it's you."

"I know, Sid. I need **_you_** to call it in for me. But you can't use my name. I can't be connected with this."

"So what's the tip?" his attorney asked him.

"There's a couple that lives next door to me. Their names are Earl and Lettie Martin, only they're pretending to be a duchess and her butler and they're running a scam. They've got all the neighborhood women involved in putting together a charity event, trying to raise funds for some phony school in Africa."

194

"I guess the women in your neighborhood must have more money than brains, huh?" Sid asked him.

Joe glanced over at Corinne and answered, "No, they're just bored and lonely."

"This hardly seems a matter of life and death," Sid told him.

"There might be more to it, though," Joe continued. "There are at least a couple of warrants out for them for pretending to be healthcare aides. They target old people who are alone and they keep them drugged while they empty their bank accounts. They're suspected of causing the death of at least one of their former 'patients'. There's a possibility that there's an old person being held hostage somewhere in that house."

"How sure are you, Joe?" Sid asked him.

"I'm not sure exactly what they're up to, but my information comes from a reliable source. And if there really are warrants out for them, that should be easy for you to check out."

"I'll make some calls after my game," Sid told him, "and see what I can do. I'll let you know how I make out."

"Here's the thing, though...their big charity event is this afternoon. I'm afraid that they'll disappear as soon as they pocket all the donations."

"Okay, I'll get right on it," Sid said. "I'll get back to you later."

Vonda, Andrew and Cassie were sitting around the fire pit waiting for their pork and rice to cook. When Vonda checked the pot and  noticed that he rice was beginning to burn, she realized that Edna May had been gone for quite a while.

"I wonder where Edna May is," she said.

"Ah...she may be napping," Andrew suggested. "She was up even earlier than usual this morning."

"Or, "Cassie added, "she could be off among the trees befriending more squirrels."

Vonda was just about to go and look for her, when Edna May came running into the camp from the direction of the bathrooms.

"Look what someone threw over the wall," she exclaimed, holding up the bottle of barbecue sauce. She poured the sauce into the pot to let the pork and rice simmer for a while until it was heated through. They all agreed that it was the best meal any of them had eaten since coming to Camp Limbo.

Will/Guillermo showed up earlier than usual that day for their last competition. He passed each camper a ping-pong paddle and three ping-pong balls. He instructed them to place their balls on the paddle and extend their arms.The first two campers to drop their balls would be in danger of elimination.They all felt pretty strong and confident going into the competition, because it would be the first time they were all competing on a full stomach.

Felicia, on the other hand, was hungry. There had been no protein bars distributed yet that day and Edna May had failed to show up at the usual time. While Edna May was concentrating on holding her paddle, Felicia was running across tree branches looking for her. She searched until she was directly over Edna May's head. She started chattering and shaking the branch until she got Edna May's attention. Edna May glanced up, saw Felicia, started laughing and dropped her balls. She was the first one out.

Vonda was determined to save herself and Edna May, and she knew that the only way to do that would be to outlast Cassie. She was sure that she could convince Andrew to vote with her, but if Cassie had a vote, she'd definitely vote to keep Andrew over Edna May. She watched Cassie out of the corner of her eye and she could see Cassie was starting to wobble. Vonda's hand was steady and she was confident that she could beat her. She would have, too, except that just as Cassie started to struggle, Ronda's water broke and Vonda felt her first labor pain, causing her to drop her balls. Andrew and Cassie were now each guaranteed a place in the final three and either Vonda or Edna May would be voted off the next day.

Andrew was torn. He had become fond of Edna May and he didn't really want to vote her off. He had a secret alliance with Vonda, though, and he didn't feel right about breaking his word to her. He asked Cassie what she thought they should do.

"I think either one of us could beat either one of them," she told him, "but I think it will be easier to beat Vonda. Edna May will probably get votes from frat-boys and porn fans. I don't think we should take that chance. If we keep Vonda, one of us is guaranteed to go home with $100,000."

Andrew really wanted to win, but he didn't really care much about the money. He had already decided to surprise his alliance and split the money with them if he did win. *What would Alex do?* he asked himself. Alex would play to win.

Joe and Corinne were having a cup of coffee on the patio when Sid called back. He and Joe talked for a few minutes and after they finished their conversation Joe hung up and told Corinne that the police were on their way.

"I gotta see this, Joe. I'll be right back," she told him and then made her way across the yard. She walked around the wall, down the hill and cut through the hedges that served as their property line in the same spot that Andrew had used earlier. She walked up to the patio, and began searching for a familiar face when she saw Amy approaching her.

"Corinne! I didn't expect to see you here," Amy told her.

"I wouldn't miss it for the world," Corinne said. "By the way, where's Oprah?"

"She's not here yet," she answered.

"Amy, she's not coming," Corinne told her.

"Yes, she definitely is," Amy replied. "I was in charge of the guest list and I saw her response card myself. She's bringing a plus one, too. I think it's Gayle."

"And what about the Kardashian? Is she not here yet either?" Corinne asked her.

"I don't know if she's coming. I never got a response from her," Amy admitted.

"She's not coming, either," Corinne told her.

"Stop it, Corinne. You're just hoping the whole thing will be a failure because you weren't involved. Look at all these people! And for your information, Brandi Glanville's sister is here and sitting on the terrace with the duchess."

"Who's Brandi Glanville?" Corinne asked.

"Geez, Corinne, do you live under a rock or something? Brandi Glanville was a 'Real Housewife'!"

"And where's the paparazzi, Amy?"

Amy pointed to a lone photographer sitting by himself at the far end of the patio. Corinne walked over to him.

"You might want to get your camera and follow me" she told him.

199

"Is Oprah finally here?" he asked her.

"No, Oprah's not coming. And neither are any other stars."

"Geez...and I was told that this was going to be some big celebrity charity event, and that I had an exclusive invitation to cover it. I missed my kid's baseball game for this. I think I'm just going to pack up my camera and go home. There's no story here."

"Oh, there's a story alright. Just not the one you were expecting," she replied.

The caterers had just finished setting up the buffet tables and a few people were lining up to eat when Corinne led the photographer across the patio, through the tree-lined path and up the stairs to the terrace. 'The Duchess' was there, sitting at one of the tables with several of her guests. She looked up as Corinne approached and said, "Corinne, I'm quite surprised to see you here. Do you understand what RSVP means?"

"I'm not here as a guest," Corinne told her. "And the real surprise is yet to come, *Lettie*."

Amy had alerted all of her friends that Corinne was there, and that she was acting strange, so they all rushed to the terrace to see what was going on.

"I think you should leave, Corinne," Lettie told her. "Unless you want me to call the police,"

"Go ahead," Corinne told her. "Call the police."

Shawna walked over to the table and grabbed Corinne's arm. "I don't know what you're trying to pull, Corinne, but I think you should leave, too. You're making a fool out of yourself and you're disrespecting the duchess. Who do you think you are?"

"Oh, I know who I am. And, I know who *she* is."

Corinne could hear sirens approaching as she turned to the crowd that was now gathered around her.

"Anyone who listed a credit card number on their donation card might want to check their account before it's too late," she told them. "Because while you're all out here eating and drinking and waiting for Oprah, Martin is probably on the computer cleaning out your accounts.

Lettie remained calm. She knew that the funds had already been transferred, and that Martin and Vickie were sitting in the car with the engine running just waiting for her to appear.

"Why, you jealous bitch," Shawna screamed at her. "Just because you don't fit in, you want to ruin it for everybody else."

"I'm not ruining anything," Corinne said. "But if you don't let go of me, I *am* gonna ruin your face."

Shawna released her grip and hissed, "Careful, Corinne. You're 'Jersey' is showing."

"Fucking A, it is," Corinne yelled. "And if you don't wanna see a Jersey girl in action, you better not put your fucking hands on me again!"

"And if you don't want to see your ass in jail," Shawna yelled back, "you'll get off Duchess Letitia's property now!"

"I'm not the one going to jail." Corinne told her. "Don't you get it? You're never going to be reimbursed for what you spent on this little soiree, and you're not going to Africa. There's no girls school. And none of you are going to have your picture taken with Oprah. You've been scammed."

Corinne turned and saw Lettie get up from her seat.

"You'll have to excuse my neighbor," Lettie told the crowd. "She often gets delusional when she forgets to take her medications. Unfortunately, this happens all too frequently. She tends to become violent, too, so if everyone would please stay here and keep her detained while I call the authorities, I'd be most grateful."

"It's too late," Corinne said as she pointed towards the door where several policemen were exiting the house.

The guests all watched in silence as Lettie was being handcuffed. Corinne positioned herself in a spot where Lettie couldn't miss seeing her as she was led away. "Aloha, *Duchess*" she said with a wave when she caught her eye. Then she turned and walked down the steps, across the patio and back through the hedges to where Joe was waiting. Maybe she'd ask him if he'd like to watch a movie and share a pizza with her.

It was mid-afternoon when the campers began to hear the sounds of voices and music coming from the other side of the wall.

"Someone must be having a party at another campsite," Andrew offered.

"Can I borrow your binoculars?" Edna May asked him. "I'm going to look for Felicia."

"Of course," he told her.

Edna May grabbed the binoculars, walked behind the bathrooms and climbed the tree. The party was in full swing and she estimated that there must be at least a hundred people there. There was a bar set up by the pool, caterers circulating with trays, several ukulele players and, of course, the pig. Or, at least, most of the pig.

The guests were starting to line up for the buffet when she began to hear sirens in the distance.

Edward Allen Milton III  heard the sirens, too. With all the other members of the household focused on packing their bags and getting ready for the party, no one had remembered to administer his 'medicine' that morning. He had a clear head for the first time in months. He prayed that the sirens were coming for him.

Chapter 23

It was the second-to-last day at Camp Limbo, and the camper's moods were mixed. Edna May and Vonda were worried, because one of them would be voted out, and Andrew was sad and depressed because he had to cast one of the votes. On the other hand, Cassie was in a great mood and she was eagerly looking forward to voting.

Inside the house, Joe was in a bad mood because his newspaper hadn't been delivered that morning. He liked to bring the paper, along with his second cup of coffee, out to the patio every morning and catch up on the news. Today was the third time this month that his paper hadn't come, and he was annoyed with the break in his routine. So he carried his coffee into the family room and turned on the local news. They were reporting live on some local event. It looked like a mob scene to Joe, and it took him a few moments to understand what he was seeing.

"Corinne," he called, "come here quick! You gotta see this."

Corinne came hurrying into the room and joined him as they watched the growing crowd outside The Bradley Motor Inn that was eagerly awaiting the last camper to be voted out of Camp Limbo. Joe was shocked at the size of the crowd, but he was even more shocked when Corinne said to him, "You can't let them bring Edna May there, if she gets voted off, Joe. That would be like shoving a lamb into a lion's den. There's always a few wackos in any crowd, and she's so vulnerable."

"I don't know what I can do about it, Corinne,"

"You can go tell the crew that she can't go. She'll have to stay here for the night."

"Are you nuts?" he asked her. "She's an ex-porn star who trespassed into our neighbor's yard and stole from them and then broke into our house to rob us, too, and you want to invite her to stay?"

"She was hungry, Joe. And she didn't 'break in'. The door wasn't even locked. And, besides, she's just a child. I mean, she's only a year older than Kara."

"And what if it's Vonda who gets voted off?" Joe asked.

"I'm pretty sure Vonda can take care of herself," she answered.


The campers were surprised to see Will/Guillermo come through the gate carrying a bouquet of light blue balloons when he arrived for the campfire meeting.

"I thought the competitions were over," Andrew said to him.

"They are," answered Will. He handed the balloons to Vonda, and told her, "Jordan LaVon Harris came into the world yesterday, just around the time that you were balancing ping-pong balls. He and his mother are both doing fine."

For the first time since she entered Camp Limbo, Vonda didn't even try to hide her emotions. "Oh my god! Oh my god!" she cried. "I'm an aunt. I have a nephew!" Andrew and Edna May were both in tears as they hugged and congratulated her.

Will lead them over to the fire pit for the campfire meeting. "Congratulations, campers," he started, "on making it to the final four. This will be the last vote before we turn it over to the viewers. Tomorrow, one of you will win the title of 'Camp Limbo Camper of the Year', along with a prize of $100,000.

"Is everyone ready to vote?" he asked them.

"Yes, we are," answered Cassie."

"Okay, let's do this. Cassie, please vote for the camper whose camping permit you would like to revoke."

"I vote for Edna May," she answered cheerfully.

"And you, Andrew?" Who would you like to see lose their permit?"

Andrew began to cry again. He took a few moments to compose himself and answered, "With great sadness, I vote for Edna May."


Edna May walked into the tent for the last time to retrieve her belongings. When she came back out Vonda and Andrew were still crying. Cassie was smiling. Edna May walked over to Andrew and hugged him. "Don't feel bad," she told him. "It's just a game. I don't have any hard feelings and I'll always consider you my friend."

"I'll see you tomorrow," Vonda said as she hugged her goodbye. "You have the address, right?"

"Yes, I've got it," Edna May assured her. "Will you do me a favor before you leave?" she asked.

"Of course. What can I do for you?"

Edna May pulled a twisted-up napkin from her backpack .She opened it up and showed Vonda the contents .She had some peanuts, a handful of stale popcorn and some pretzel pieces left over from one of the competitions.

"We you give these to Felicia?"

"Sure, sweetheart. I promise."


And then Edna May walked out of Joe's backyard and into his home.


The voting option on the Camp Limbo website was enabled as soon as Edna May walked out the gate.The response was much greater than the crew had anticipated, causing the site to crash twice. Twenty-four hours after Edna May walked out through the Camp Limbo gate, Will/Guillermo walked in with the voting results. The campers were already sitting around the fire pit waiting for him.They had spent the morning eating the remaining rice and protein bars and packing their backpacks.

"Buenos Dias, campers," he greeted them. "I have the voting results here in my hand."

Will made a big show of opening the sealed envelope. He read the results to himself before announcing, " And.....the camper who received the least amount of votes, and will be the sixth camper to have their permit revoked is....Cassie.

"Cassie, please pick up your backpack and wait by the gate."

Cassie snorted and said to Andrew "I think this whole thing was rigged! There's no way she got more votes than I did."

Will ignored her comment and waited for her to walk away. There were no tearful goodbyes. When she had reached the gate, Will turned to the final two campers and said, "And the winner of the Camp Limbo 'Camper of the Year" award is…...Congratulations, Vonda!"

Joe, Corinne and Edna May were gathered around the kitchen table watching the finale together on Joe's laptop. "I'm glad it wasn't Cassie," Corinne said.

"Yeah, me too," Joe agreed.

"Me too," Edna May added.

While one crew member drove the blindfolded campers around before depositing them back in the parking garage, Will and the rest of them began to dismantle Camp Limbo. They took the tent down, filled in the fire pit and mowed what was left of the lawn. When Will returned the riding mower to the garage, Joe was waiting for him.

"You guys did a great job," he told him. "I know you're not allowed to make money on the project, so I've got a proposition for you. I'd like to pay your tuition for next semester. You made me a lot of money and I'd like to repay you somehow."

"Thanks, Mr. B. I appreciate it," Will answered. "but I'm taking next semester off. I've been offered a great opportunity that I just can't turn down. I'm going to be on 'Dancing With The Stars'."

"You're kidding! That's great. I didn't know you were a dancer."

"I'm not a dancer. They give you lessons, though," Will told him.

"So what star will you be dancing with? Do you know?" Joe asked him.

"I *am* the star, Mr. B. Well, actually Guillermo is the star. But I'm Guillermo, right?"

"But Guillermo's just a character," Joe reminded him. "He's not real."

Will laughed and added, "Haven't you realized yet, Mr. B., that there's nothing real about reality shows?"

Chapter 24

Joe was sitting on the patio the next morning, drinking his coffee and reading the paper when Corinne came looking for him. "There's something I want to talk to you about," she said.

"Shoot," he said and put the paper aside.

"Would you be real upset if I told you that I want to sell the house?" she asked him.

"But I thought you loved this house," he told her.

"I do love the house. Well, except for the kitchen," she added. "But I don't love the lifestyle. Or the neighborhood. Or most of the neighbors, for that matter. "I want to move back, Joe. Back to a place where I feel comfortable. I'm sorry to spring this on you, but I've been wanting to go back for a while now."

"You want to go back to Jersey?" he asked, surprised by the idea.

"No! God, no. I want to go back to our last neighborhood. I'm sorry, Joe, but I just don't really like it here. I hope you're not upset."

"Corinne, remember when we were in high school and we used to go to the shore all the time?" he asked her.

"Of course, I remember," she told him.

"Do you remember that time we rented a boat and rode it down to that spot with all the mansions? We were fantasizing about what it would be like to live in one of them. Remember?"

Corinne nodded.

"Well, I've wanted to buy you your dream house ever since that day. I might not be able to afford one of those oceanside mansions, but this….." Joe moved his arm to indicate he meant the house, "...this ain't bad."

"But I was a kid then, Joe. That's not what I want anymore." she told him.

"Oh, I know that," he told her. "But the point is, I *can* buy you your dream house. And that's what makes me happy. So, yeah, if this isn't it, and you want to move, we'll move."

"Thanks for understanding, Joe."

"And to tell you the truth," Joe went on, "I don't like it here any more than you do."

"So we can start looking as soon as your sentence is over?" she asked him.

"We don't have to wait. I'll call the realtor tomorrow and tell her what we're looking for. You can go see them without me. I trust your judgment. We'll need a big kitchen......"

"One that doesn't need to be updated." Corinne added.

"....Yeah, and open to the family room. I need an office and we'll need what? Four or five bedrooms?"

"At least six," Corinne told him.

"Six? How many guest rooms do we need?" he asked.

"We only need one guest room," she told him, "but Maria and Alfie will each need their own rooms."

"Maria and Alfie are coming with us?" he asked her.

"Of course, Joe. Where else would they go?"

# PART FIVE

# REALITY

Chapter 25

The blindfolds went back on as the four campers were led to the van that would deliver them to their cars. The last campers to leave Camp Limbo were allowed to travel together. There was no longer any reason to keep them apart. When they finally arrived at the parking garage, Cassie pitched a fit and refused to get out.

"It's only fair," she complained to Emma, their driver. "I want my room at The Bradley Inn and I want my $100. That's what everyone else got. I still have an hour and a half drive home and I want to take a shower, put on clean clothes and get something to eat first."

She was so persistent, that Emma pulled the car into a parking spot and dialed Will's cellphone. Will was in the studio apartment with Joe and a couple of the other crew members, where they were in the process of dismantling the control room.

"Let her have it," Joe told Will when he explained the situation. "It's only fair. What about the other three?" he asked. They want rooms too?"

"The other three just want to get in their cars and go home," Will answered.

Cassie checked into her room, showered, put on clean clothes and ordered room service. When she had finished her meal she called the front desk and requested that the their transportation service drive her to her car.

"The next courtesy van leaves at 6 AM tomorrow morning, ma'am," she was told. "Would you like a wake-up call?"

"No, I would *not* like a wake-up call. I would like a ride to my car and I would like it now."

"I'm sorry, ma'am,' the clerk answered, "but that's just not possible."

"It's an emergency," Cassie told her. "My mother is very ill and I need to get home as soon as possible."

"I'd be happy to summon a cab for you, if you'd like."

Cassie snorted, and said, "No, I would **not** *like* a cab. But I guess if that's the best you can do, I'll take it. I can assure you, though, that neither I, nor any member of my family will ever step foot in The Bradley Inn again!"

"Okay, ma'am," the clerk said. "I'll have a cab waiting for you in ten minutes. You have a nice day now and thank you for choosing The Bradley Inn as your home away from home."

When Cassie entered the front door of her home she was surprised to hear voices coming from the family room, because she thought her parents would be gone for the whole month. She was even more surprised when she found her sister and her nephews sitting on the couch watching TV.

"Cassie," Linda exclaimed when she saw her, "what are you doing here?"

"What am *I* doing here? I live here," she answered  "What are *you* doing here?"

"I'm house-sitting for Mom and Dad," Linda told her.  "How was your camping trip?"

"It was absolutely brutal," she answered. "I had to sleep on the ground in a tent! There were no showers or indoor plumbing at all and hardly any food."

"I'm not surprised that you didn't enjoy it," Linda told her. "I never pegged you for a camper."

"It wasn't a camping trip, Linda," Cassie explained. "It was a reality show. Didn't Mom explain it to you?"

"No," Linda answered her. "She just said you went camping. So, when is the show supposed to air?"

"It has *already* aired. It was a live web show. I can't believe Mom didn't tell you!"

"Was it like 'Survivor'?" Linda asked.

"Yes, exactly," Cassie replied. "The conditions were horrible and so were the other contestants. I had to share the tent with a couple of 'bro' types and an actual porn-star. Can you believe it? A porn-star!"

"Oh my god!" Linda exclaimed. "You were on 'Camp Limbo! Tell me...what's she really like?"

"What's who like?" Cassie asked.

"The porn star. Edna May. I read about her in 'People' or 'In Touch', magazine. And, of course, I heard about the crowd that gathered at The Bradley Inn to greet her when she got voted off."

"I was brought to that same hotel, Linda. There were no crowds. Just a couple of bloggers looking for interviews."

"It was on the news, Cassie," Linda told her. "There were so many people there that they had to bring in police to direct traffic. It was so crazy that they ended up bringing her someplace secret.

"So, tell me,...What is she really like?"

"I didn't get to know her very well," Cassie said. "She's a porn star, for crying out loud. I had absolutely nothing in common with her. There was only one other contestant that I had anything in common with. His name is Andrew and he's an author and a teacher. He's an amazing guy."

"It sounds like maybe sparks were flying," Linda teased.

"Definitely. We could hardly stay away from each other. Unfortunately, he's stuck in an unhappy marriage."

"Oh, Cassie...that's what they all say."

"No, he never actually said that," Cassie corrected her. "He's much too loyal and honorable to air his dirty laundry in public. You can just tell. I could see that he wasn't looking forward to going home to that horrid woman."

"You met her?" Linda asked.

"No," Cassie answered, "but I did see a picture of her. Oh, Linda, she looks like Barbara Bush. And not the cute twin....the *late* Barbara Bush."

"So did you win anything?" Linda asked.

"Yes, actually, I did. I won exactly $100, most of which I spent on not-so-fine-dining and cabfare. Of course, you'd know all this if you had watched.

"I'll be in my room," she told her sister and stomped up the stairs. When she entered her bedroom she slammed the door with a loud bang. She reappeared in the family room a few seconds later.

"Where is my mattress?" she demanded.

"Oh, I'm sorry, Cassie," Linda said. "It's on the patio. Airing out. Jake had a little accident last night."

"How could you let him do that?"

"I didn't *let* him, Linda answered. "He must've had a nightmare or something.
But you can sleep in my old room or the spare room tonight. I'll bring two of the boys into Mom and Dad's bedroom with me."

"No," Cassie replied. "I will *not* sleep in your old room or in the spare room either. I'm sleeping in my own room tonight and in my own bed. If you were able to move my mattress to the patio, then you're more than capable of moving another mattress onto my bed."

After Cassie's room was put back together to her satisfaction she called her Mom on her cell phone.

"Hi, Mom," she greeted her. "I'm home."

"And how was your camping trip?" her mother asked. "Did you have a good time?"

"It was tough, Mom. I'm sure you could tell by watching the show."

"No, honey. I didn't see any of it. You know I'm not very proficient on the computer. The most I know how to do is read my emails."

"But I showed you how to do it, Mom! I can't believe you didn't watch me."

"Well, I am on vacation. I sure didn't want to spend my time in front of the computer. I promise I'll watch it when it comes on television. Can you set the DVR for me?"

"It's not going to be on TV, Mom. It was a live web show," Cassie explained.

"I thought you said it was a pilot. Maybe it will get picked up by one of the networks and then we'll be able to watch it on TV."

"No, we won't. It's a reality show, mother, where people get voted out and the last person standing is the winner, which wasn't me but should have been. If the pilot gets picked up, they'll have a whole new cast."

"Well, I don't know why," her mother told her. "If it does get picked up, maybe they'll invite you back and you'll have another chance to win. There's a houseguest on 'Big Brother' this summer who was also on last year. They bring back contestants from other seasons all the time."

"You watched Big Brother, but you didn't watch me?" Cassie fumed.

Cassie hung up on her mother and crawled into bed.She had been looking forward to sleeping in her own bed for the last three weeks, but now that she was here, she found that she couldn't fall asleep. She wished she could talk to Andrew. She missed him and felt that he must be missing her, too. She got out of bed and went and sat at her desk. She turned her computer on and logged into Facebook. She sent Andrew a friend request and then went back to bed and fell asleep. He never responded.

Chapter 26

Andrew returned home from Camp Limbo and found that his house key no longer worked. Nan had hired a locksmith to change the locks while Andrew was away. She wanted a divorce and offered him a generous sum of money, provided that he go quickly and quietly. That wasn't a problem, as she had already packed his bags. Andrew's idea of appearing on a reality show to promote his book turned out to be a good one. His book sold briskly during the first week of Camp Limbo, but sales came to a halt after the first few reviews were posted. He was disappointed, but not crushed. He decided that he just wasn't meant to be a novelist. His mother had always told him that he had the soul of a poet, and he felt that maybe his writing talents lie in that direction.

He started going to open mic poetry readings. He didn't go to present his own work, because he had no work to show. He went so that he could study other poets' performances and see how audiences responded. There was one particular poet who interested him the most. She was a transgender woman who called herself 'Cinderella', Cindy to her friends. Andrew found her poems to be so honest and raw that her readings sometimes brought him to tears. Her performances made him realize, however, that he'd never be a real poet. He thought maybe he should consider writing short stories. He kept attending poetry readings to hear Cinderella, and eventually worked up the nerve to approach her and introduce himself.

"I know who you are," she told him."You're Wordman."

They were engaged two months later.

Some of the online celebrity gossip sites found out about the impending wedding and posted articles about the couple. A few days after the notices appeared, Cindy received a call from a woman who worked in the production office of *Say Yes To The Dress.*

"We'd like to feature you in an upcoming episode," the woman told her. "We'll give you 20% off of any dress in the store along with the opportunity to promote your latest book and represent your community to a large audience."

"I like that idea," Cindy answered. "There's still so much misunderstanding about the LGBTQ community and…."

"No, no. That's not what I meant," the woman cut her off. "We've had plenty of lesbian and transgender brides on the show. No offense, but that's *so* last year."

"So are you talking about the Samoan-American community?" Cindy asked, surprised.

"No, not that, either," she answered. "We've had brides from every ethnic and minority group that you can think of. We've also had athletes, soldiers, country singers, rock stars and little people. We've had disaster survivors, nurses, ministers and paraplegics. Frankly, we're running out of ideas, which is why we're coming to you. We've never had a poet. Or poetess. Which do you prefer?"

"Poet will do just fine," she answered. 'It's an intriguing offer, but I'm not sure that I want anyone to see me in my dress before I walk down the aisle."

"That won't be a problem," the woman continued, " because we never air the episodes until after the wedding"

"Can you make it 30% plus travel expenses?" Cindy asked.

"The best I can do is 25% plus plane fare for you and a guest."

"Well then I'm saying 'yes' to the dress!"

When Edna May learned from Sam that Joe had completed his sentence and was trying to build up his business, she convinced Cindy and Andrew to hire him as their wedding photographer. She never told Andrew that Joe had anything to do with Camp Limbo, but she had told Vonda the whole story.

The wedding was held in the banquet hall at the Bradley Inn. The room opened onto a private courtyard where the staff set up rows of chairs for guests to witness the outdoor ceremony. Afterwards they'd go inside for dinner and dancing. Extra security had been hired to keep out wedding crashers and paparazzi. They were stationed at the entrances that led from the lobby to the private room.

Cassie was in that same lobby, hiding behind a potted plant while she waited for an opportunity to enter the ballroom. She watched while Vonda and Edna May were let in and then she attached herself to a group of four people approaching the door. The others each handed a card to the guard and were allowed in.

"I have an invitation, too," she told the guard, "but I forgot to bring it."

"Name?" he asked her.

She gave him her name and waited while he checked the guest list.

"Your name's not on the list," he told her when he looked up. "I can't let you in."

"There must be some kind of mistake," she answered indignantly. "I explained to you that I have an invitation, but I forgot it. Are you calling me a liar?"

"Sorry, ma'am, but I'm going to have to ask you to leave. You're not on the list."

"I *demand* to speak to Andrew," she yelled. "He's the groom, by the way, and a close, personal friend of mine. If he finds out that you've barred me from his wedding, you'll be sorry."

"I know who he is, ma'am. But you're still not on the list. And if you don't calm down and leave quietly, I'm going to have to call the police."

"But I *need* to get in there before they say 'I do'," she wailed. "He's making a mistake. Again! I 'googled' her...SHE'S A MAN! I have to warn him...."

Cassie was still yelling, "SHE'S A MAN," as the police escorted her out of the building. One guest was lucky enough to capture the whole scene on video and submit the tape to *America's Funniest Home Videos*, winning himself $10,000.

With permission from Andrew and Cinderella, Joe was able to sell some of his photographs of the wedding to the tabloids. And while the pictures didn't make him famous, they did give his business a huge boost and brought him steady work.

When Vonda and Edna May found out that Guillermo was going to be a contestant on 'Dancing With The Stars', they invited Andrew and Cinderella to join them each week to have dinner together while watching the show. It was during one of their dinners that Andrew made an announcement.

"We want you to be the first to know," he told them, "we're going to be parents."

"Congratulations!" Edna May said. "I'm so happy for you guys."

"I don't mean to be rude," Vonda told them, "but just how is that going to happen?"

"Were going to be foster parents," Cinderella explained. "We start training next week."

"And it's all because of you," Andrew told Edna May. "Your story inspired us. We'd like to share our home with children who are missing out on the family life and love they deserve."

"That means a lot to me," Edna May told him. "There are so many kids out there that need it. I never had a real abusive foster family, but I never had one where I felt loved, either. You guys will be great foster parents. I'm so proud of you."

"Yeah, me, too," Vonda added. "It's what Alex would do."

Chapter 27

Joe, Corinne, Maria and Alfie were gathered around the television in the family room of their new home. They were watching the season finale of 'Dancing With The Stars'. Will/Guillermo and his partner had made the final two. They had danced a pasa doble for their last performance, and when the music ended, Will bowed to the judges and ripped off his mask. The audience loved it, and Joe had been convinced that Will would take home the trophy. He was    shocked and disappointed when the host read the results and Will had taken second place.

"Geez," Joe said, "I thought he nailed it."

"Me, too," Corinne agreed. "But that girl's pretty popular. She used to be on TV in one of those teen soaps. I think she played a vampire or a witch or something."

"But she fell," Joe complained.

"I know, but it's not about who's better. It's about who has the most fans," Corinne told him.

"Well, I still think that Will, or Guillermo, or whatever he's calling himself should have won..."

"Shhh," Corinne said and pointed back to the television, "look at that."

Joe looked back at the screen to see a promo for a new show was airing. The scene showed a group of four males and four females sitting around a campfire and throwing peanuts to a giant squirrel while a voice announced, "A new sitcom from the creators of 'Angie Tribeca', and based on the web sensation of the same name... It's 'Camp Limbo'. Not quite heaven, not quite hell. Tuesdays at 8:30, 7:30 Central.

Nikki had watched the finale, too, but had changed the channel before the commercial for 'Camp Limbo' aired. There was a new episode of 'Tiny Houses' coming on, and she didn't want to miss it. She listened as the familiar voice at the beginning of the show recited the opening remarks for that episode, "Newly divorced Zeke and his friend Justin, are

230

searching for a tiny house that will accommodate their bachelor lifestyles, but won't break the bank."

She changed the channel and watched a rerun of *The Big Bang Theory*. She was starting to fall asleep when she heard the sound of a key unlocking the apartment door. She rushed to the door and was standing with her hands on her hips when it opened.

"Where the hell have you been," she asked.

"I went for a beer run, babe," came the reply.

"I told you..Don't call me that!" she hissed. "A beer run? You've been gone for two hours. What were you doing for two hours?"

"I stopped at the bar on the corner. They had a card game going in the back room, so I played a few hands. I won fifty dollars."

"Great. Fifty bucks. That will really help us get out of this dump. Maybe you should get a real job. Then maybe we can get a real home."

"I thought you liked tiny living?"

"I want a tiny house, you moron. Not this stupid studio apartment. Do you ever listen to me? Do you even care what I want? Does *anybody* care about me?" she asked him.

"Of course, Nikki. Jesus loves you."

"Fuck you, Kyle."

Joe called Will a few days later to congratulate him on his performance.

"I thought you did a great job, Will. I thought you deserved the win."

"Thanks, Mr. B. A lot of people are telling me the same thing. I had a great time, though. I can't complain.

"Oh, and I saw Edna May recently," he added.

"Yeah," Joe said, "me, too. I see her commercials all the time."

"No, I mean I ran into her. I actually bought a car from her."

"Really? You bought a car from her? Sam told me that so many people came to the lot looking to buy a car from her, that he made her a sales person. What kind did you get?"

"I got a Lexus. It's a few years old, but it sure is sweet."

"I guess 'Dancing With The Stars' pays pretty good," Joe remarked.

"No, not really," Will told him. "I've been making money doing personal appearances."

"What do you mean by 'personal appearances'?" Joe asked him.

"I get invited to go to things like parties, premiers and other celebrity events. I just have to show up as Guillermo and schmooze a little and I get paid. And the swag bags are incredible."

"Wow, that's great. Anyway," Joe continued, "I was calling to let you know that my offer still stands. I wanted to pay for your next semester of school, although it sounds like you're doing okay."

"Thanks, Mr. B, but I'm not going back," Will told him. "I got another gig… I'm going to be the next 'Bachelor'."

"You're kidding! I didn't even know you and your girlfriend broke up."

"We didn't, but she's cool. She knows it's just for my career. Besides, it's not like I'll be cheating or anything. I'll just be acting."

"But I thought 'The Bachelor' was supposed to be real. I thought it was a reality show," Joe said.

"It is, Mr. B. But like I keep telling you, there's nothing real about reality shows."

# The End

Made in the USA
Middletown, DE
20 February 2020